SHADOWS OVER ELDORIA

BOOK:1 OF CHRONICALS OF ELDORIA

ANSHIKA PALO

To my dear Sunshine and Moonlight,

Contents

Preface

On the eve of Christmas, as snowflakes pirouette through the twilight sky, 13-year-old Yuna's life takes an extraordinary turn. In the heart of Willowbend, a quaint village nestled between emerald meadows and frost-kissed woodlands, she hums softly while kneading dough in the villages warm, spice-scented kitchen. But as the twilight deepens into a velvety indigo, a mysterious letter flutters onto the windowsill—a summons from the illustrious Celestial Council. Within its gilded pages lies an invitation to a destiny far grander than she could have ever imagined.

Accompanied by her steadfast companions— Callum and the valiant, ever-loyal Kael—Yuna embarks on a journey beyond the world she knows, stepping into a realm woven with enchantment. Through spectral forests where the trees murmur ancient secrets and crystalline lakes reflect hidden truths, they traverse landscapes both breathtaking and perilous. A sagacious, silver-barked tree whispers riddles of forgotten lore, while shadowy phantoms prowl in the periphery, heralding the arrival of an ominous force that seeks to unravel the very fabric of existence.

As Yuna unearths the long-buried mysteries of her lineage, she must awaken the power slumbering within her soul. But magic alone is not enough—courage must temper her fear, friendship must fortify her resolve, and belief in herself must illuminate the path ahead. The darkness looms ever closer, its tendrils clawing at the edges of their world. With time slipping through her fingers like grains of stardust, will Yuna rise to the fate etched in the constellations before all is lost?

CHAPTER I

The Letter

Yuna Celestia lived a simple life in the quaint village of Willowbend, where rolling hills met the edge of the vast Eldorian Forest. The thatched roofs of the village cottages blended seamlessly into the landscape, and the air was sweet with the scent of blooming wildflowers. It was a place where time stood still, where the rhythms of nature dictated the pace of life, and where everyone knew each other's names.

She marched down the dew- filled streets of willowbend for helping the villagers with the Christmas Eve decoration. Now the sun was at it's highest point, Smiling brightly at the children and Women baking aromatic pies and delicious choclate filled pastries. Everyone was in a Merry mood exept Yuna she felt like something unexpected was about to happen.

Twilight sprinkled Yuna with some merryness while she sat down the corner surrounded by children who used to come every year to hear stories from Yuna's Old grandma who she lived with. She then saw a hooded figure signalling her to come. Feeling nervous she went and received the parchment that gleamed with an ancient seal, and as she traced her fingers over the intricate design, a sense of destiny enveloped her. The seal depicted a stylized image of a crescent moon, surrounded by stars and vines, and it seemed to shimmer in the morning light. Yuna's heart skipped a beat as she turned the parchment over, her eyes scanning the address: "Yuna Celestia, Willowbend Village." The handwriting was elegant, with flourishes and curves that seemed to dance across the page.

Yuna's hands trembled slightly as she broke the seal, the wax cracking with a soft snap. She unfolded the parchment, and a musty scent wafted up, carrying with it whispers of forgotten knowledge. The letter was written in a language she didn't recognize, the script flowing like a river of gold across the page. But as she touched the parchment, the words began to shift, rearranging themselves into a language she could understand.

The message was brief, consisting of only a few lines:

"Yuna Celestia, daughter of the moon, Your presence is requested at the Celestial Conclave. Come alone, and come prepared, For the fate of the realms hangs in the balance.

—A friend"

Yuna's mind reeled as she read the words, her thoughts racing with questions. What was the Celestial Conclave? Who was the mysterious sender, and how did they know her name? The phrase "daughter of the moon" sent a shiver down her spine, for it was a title she had heard only in whispers, spoken by the village elder in hushed tones.

As she stood there, the letter trembling in her hands, Yuna felt the world around her begin to shift. The familiar rhythms of the village, the comforting routines of her daily life, all seemed to fade into the background. A sense of restlessness stirred within her, a feeling that she was being called to something greater, something that lay beyond the boundaries of Willowbend. The village was quiet, the only sound the distant clucking of chickens and the soft rustle of leaves in the breeze. Yuna's cottage, with its thatched roof and smoke drifting lazily from the chimney, seemed to shrink, becoming smaller and more insignificant with each passing moment. She felt a sudden urge to leave, to walk away from the only life she had ever known and into the unknown.

With the letter still clutched in her hand, Yuna turned to face the Eldorian Forest, its trees towering above the village like sentinels. The forest was a place of mystery and wonder, a realm of ancient magic and forgotten lore. As she gazed into its depths, Yuna felt an inexplicable pull, a sense that the forest was calling to her, drawing her into its shadows.

The sun was climbing below in the sky, casting a cold shiver over the village. Yuna's stomach growled, reminding her that she had skipped dinner the night before, lost in the pages of an old book she had found in the village library. But as she stood there, the letter still clutched in her hand, Yuna knew that she couldn't eat, not now, not when her world was changing so profoundly. She felt a sense of disconnection, as if she was floating above her body, watching herself from afar. The letter had awakened something within her, a spark that had been smoldering, waiting to be fanned into a flame.

With a sense of determination, Yuna folded the parchment and tucked it into her pocket. She knew that she had to leave, to follow the call of the unknown, no matter where it might lead. The Celestial Conclave, the mysterious sender, the fate of the realms – all these things swirled in her mind, a maelstrom of questions and doubts. But as she turned to face the forest, Yuna felt a sense of clarity, a sense that she was being drawn into a larger world, a world of wonder and magic. The trees seemed to loom closer, their branches reaching out like arms, embracing her. The wind rustled through the leaves, whispering secrets in a language she couldn't quite understand.

And then, with a sense of purpose, Yuna set off towards the forest, the letter clutched in her hand, her heart pounding with excitement and fear. She didn't know what lay ahead, but she was ready to face it, to follow the call of the unknown, no matter where it might lead. As she walked, the village fell away behind her, the thatched roofs and the smoke drifting from the chimneys growing smaller and smaller. The forest loomed closer, its trees towering above her, casting dappled shadows on the ground. Yuna felt a sense of freedom, a sense that she was leaving behind the familiar routines of her life and embarking on a journey into the unknown.

The trees seemed to close in around her, their branches tangling above her head, forming a canopy of leaves and shadows. The air was cool and damp, filled with the scent of moss and earth. Yuna breathed deeply, feeling the forest's energy coursing through her veins. She had always loved the forest, had spent countless hours exploring its secrets, but now, with the letter clutched in her hand, she felt a sense of purpose, a sense that she was being drawn into a larger world.

As she walked, the trees grew taller, their trunks thicker, their branches more twisted. The forest floor was carpeted with a soft layer of moss and leaves, and the sound of running water grew louder, a gentle melody that seemed to accompany her on her journey. Yuna felt a sense of peace, a sense that she was being guided, that the forest was leading her towards her destiny. Yuna walked for hours, the trees blurring together, their branches merging into a seamless whole. She felt a sense of timelessness as if she had been walking for centuries as if the forest was eternal, and she was just a fleeting moment in its history.

And then, as the sun was in its twlight it glowed, casting a golden glow over the forest, Yuna came to a clearing. In the center of the clearing stood an enormous tree, its trunk twisted and gnarled, its branches reaching towards the sky like a giant's fist. The tree seemed to pulse with energy, its bark glowing with a soft, ethereal light. Yuna felt a sense of awe, a sense that she was standing in the presence of something ancient and powerful. She approached the tree slowly, her heart pounding with excitement and fear. As she reached out to touch the trunk, the tree seemed to stir, its branches rustling softly.

And then, in a voice that was both familiar and strange, the tree spoke to her, its words echoing in her mind. "Welcome, Yuna Celestia," it said. "I have been waiting for you. You have been called to the Celestial Conclave, a gathering of the ancient ones, the guardians of the realms. You have a role to play in the fate of the worlds, a role that only you can fulfill."

Yuna's mind reeled as she listened to the tree's words. She felt a sense of wonder, a sense that she was being drawn into a world of magic and mystery. The tree's words seemed to awaken something within her, a spark that had been smoldering, waiting to be fanned into a flame. And then, with a sense of determination, Yuna replied, "I am ready. I will follow the call of the unknown, no matter where it may lead." The tree seemed to nod, its branches rustling softly. "Then let us begin," it said. "The journey to the Celestial Conclave is long and fraught with danger. But with courage and determination, you will succeed. You will fulfill your destiny, and the fate of the realms will be decided."

As the tree finished speaking, the forest seemed to come alive. The trees rustled and swayed, their branches tangling together in a intricate pattern. The air was filled with a soft, ethereal glow, and Yuna felt herself being lifted out of her body, transported to a realm beyond the physical world.

She saw visions of ancient civilizations, of mighty kingdoms and powerful magic. She saw the threads of fate that connected all things, the delicate balance of the universe. And she saw herself, standing at the center of it all, a key player in the drama that was unfolding. The vision faded, and Yuna found herself back in the clearing, the tree looming above her. She felt a sense of wonder, a sense that she had been given a glimpse of a larger world, a world of magic and mystery. And she knew that she was ready, ready to embark on the journey to the Celestial Conclave, ready to fulfill her destiny and decide the fate of the realms.

With a sense of purpose, Yuna set off towards the unknown, the tree's words echoing in her mind. She walked for hours, the forest blurring together, the trees merging into a seamless whole. She felt a sense of timelessness as if she had been walking for centuries as if the forest was eternal, and she was just a fleeting moment in its history. And then, as the sun began to set, casting a golden glow over the forest, Yuna came to a river. The water was crystal clear, reflecting the sky above like a mirror. A small boat was waiting for her, its hull adorned with intricate carvings of moons and stars.

Yuna felt a sense of wonder, a sense that she was being guided, that the universe was conspiring to help her on her journey. She climbed into the boat, feeling the wood beneath her feet, the gentle rocking of the vessel as it floated on the water. As she pushed off from the shore, the boat began to move, gliding smoothly across the river. Yuna felt a sense of peace, a sense that she was being carried towards her destiny. The forest blurred together, the trees merging into a seamless whole, as the boat drifted downstream.

The sun dipped completely below the horizon, casting a golden glow over the water. Yuna felt a sense of magic, a sense that she was being transported to a world beyond the physical realm. The stars began to twinkle in the sky above, and the moon rose, casting a silver glow over the river.

As the boat drifted on, Yuna felt herself becoming one with the universe, her spirit merging with the cosmos. She saw visions of the past and the future, the threads of fate that connected all things. And she saw herself, standing at the center of it all, a key player in the drama that was unfolding.

The vision faded, and Yuna found herself back in the boat, the river flowing smoothly beneath her. She felt a sense of wonder, a sense that she had been given a glimpse of a larger world, a world of magic and mystery. And she knew that she was ready, ready to embark on the journey to the Celestial Conclave, ready to fulfill her destiny and decide the fate of the realms.

As the boat drifted on, Yuna felt a sense of excitement, a sense that she was being carried towards her destiny. The river wound its way through the forest, the trees looming above her like sentinels. The air was filled with the scent of blooming flowers, and the sound of birds singing in the trees.

And then, as the sun began to rise, casting a golden glow over the forest, Yuna saw it – a shimmering city, its towers and spires reaching towards the sky like a giant's fist. The city seemed to pulse with energy, its walls glowing with a soft, ethereal light. Yuna felt a sense of awe, a sense that she was standing in the presence of something ancient and powerful. She knew that she had reached the end of her journey, that the Celestial Conclave was waiting for her. And with a sense of determination, she stepped out of the boat, her feet touching the shore.

The city loomed above her, its towers and spires reaching towards the sky. Yuna felt a sense of wonder, a sense that she was being drawn into a world of magic and mystery. And she knew that she was ready, ready to fulfill her destiny, ready to decide the fate of the realms.

As she walked towards the city, the gates swung open, revealing a world of wonder and magic. Yuna felt a sense of excitement, a sense that she was being drawn into a realm beyond the physical world. And she knew that she was ready, ready to embark on the journey of a lifetime, ready to fulfill her destiny and decide the fate of the realms. The city was filled with strange and wondrous creatures, beings of light and shadow, magic and mystery. Yuna felt a sense of wonder, a sense that she was being introduced to a world beyond her wildest dreams. And she knew that she was ready—ready to learn, ready to grow, ready to fulfill her destiny.

As she walked through the city, Yuna saw marvels beyond her imagination. She saw towers that seemed to touch the sky, gardens filled with flowers that shone like stars, and fountains that flowed with water that seemed like liquid moonlight. And she knew that she was ready, ready to explore, ready to discover, ready to fulfill her destiny. The city was filled with ancient wisdom, with secrets and mysteries that had been hidden for centuries. Yuna felt a sense of awe, a sense that she was being initiated into a world of magic and wonder. And she knew that she was ready, ready to learn, ready to grow, ready to fulfill her destiny.

As she walked through the city, Yuna came to a great hall, its ceiling lost in the shadows. The hall was filled with beings of light and shadow, creatures of magic and mystery. And at the far end of the hall, on a throne of crystal and silver, sat a figure of great power and wisdom. Yuna felt a sense of awe, a sense that she was standing in the presence of something ancient and powerful. The figure on the throne seemed to pulse with energy, its presence filling the hall with a soft, ethereal glow. And Yuna knew that she was ready, ready to meet her destiny, ready to fulfill her role in the drama that was unfolding.

The figure on the throne spoke, its voice like thunder in Yuna's mind. "Welcome, Yuna Celestia," it said. "You have been called to the Celestial Conclave, a gathering of the ancient ones, the guardians of the realms. You have a role to play in the fate of the worlds, a role that only you can fulfill."

Yuna felt a sense of wonder, a sense that she was being drawn into a world of magic and mystery. She knew that she was ready, ready to embark on the journey of a lifetime, ready to fulfill her destiny and decide the fate of the realms. And with a sense of determination, she replied, "I am ready. I will fulfill my destiny, and I will decide the fate of the realms." The figure on the throne nodded, its presence filling the hall with a soft, ethereal glow. "Then let us begin," it said. "The journey to the Celestial Conclave is long and fraught with danger. But with courage and determination, you will succeed. You will fulfill your destiny, and the fate of the realms will be decided."

As the figure finished speaking, the hall seemed to come alive. The beings of light and shadow, the creatures of magic and mystery, all seemed to stir, their presence filling the hall with a soft, ethereal glow. Yuna felt a sense of wonder, a sense that she was being drawn into a world of magic and mystery. And she knew that she was ready, ready to embark on the journey of a lifetime, ready to fulfill her destiny and decide the fate of the realms.

The journey to the Celestial Conclave had begun, and Yuna was ready. She was ready to face whatever challenges lay ahead, ready to fulfill her destiny, and ready to decide the fate of the realms. The adventure had started, and Yuna was eager to see what lay ahead. As Yuna stood before the figure on the throne, she felt a sense of trepidation. She knew that the journey to the Celestial Conclave would be difficult, that she would face challenges and dangers at every turn. But she also knew that she was ready, ready to face whatever lay ahead, ready to fulfill her destiny.

The figure on the throne spoke again, its voice like thunder in Yuna's mind. "The journey to the Celestial Conclave is long and fraught with danger," it said. "But with courage and determination, you will succeed. You will fulfill your destiny, and the fate of the realms will be decided."

Yuna felt a sense of determination, a sense that she was ready to face whatever lay ahead. She knew that the journey would be difficult, but she also knew that she was ready, ready to fulfill her destiny and decide the fate of the realms. As she stood before the figure on the throne, Yuna felt a sense of wonder. She knew that she was being drawn into a world of magic and mystery, a world of ancient wisdom and forgotten lore. And she knew that she was ready, ready to learn, ready to grow, ready to fulfill her destiny.

The figure on the throne spoke again, its voice like thunder in Yuna's mind. "You will face many challenges on your journey," it said. "You will face dangers and difficulties, but you must not be afraid. You must be brave, and you must be determined. You must fulfill your destiny, and you must decide the fate of the realms."

Yuna felt a sense of courage, a sense that she was ready to face whatever lay ahead. She knew that the journey would be difficult, but she also knew that she was ready, ready to fulfill her destiny and decide the fate of the realms. As she stood before the figure on the throne, Yuna felt a sense of awe. She knew that she was being drawn into a world of magic and mystery, a world of ancient wisdom and forgotten lore. And she knew that she was ready, ready to learn, ready to grow, ready to fulfill her destiny.

The figure on the throne spoke again, its voice like thunder in Yuna's mind. "You will meet many people on your journey," it said. "You will meet friends and allies,

CHAPTER II

A New Beginning

And magically she reached in a carriage that lurched to a final, groaning stop, the worn leather of its cushions sighing in relief. Yuna, her stomach doing a nervous somersault that had nothing to do with the bumpy ride, peered out the window. The sight that greeted her stole her breath and did little to calm her fluttering heart. She saw that the prestigious Arcanum Academy wasn't just a school; but a monument to magic itself. Towering spires of obsidian and shimmering quartz pierced the sky, their tips swirling with faint, ethereal light. Each tower was different, adorned with intricate carvings of arcane symbols and mythical creatures. Some were smooth and sleek, others jagged and imposing, yet they all seemed to hum with an inner power. Around the base of these majestic structures sprawled a tapestry of enchanted gardens. Flowers of every hue imaginable bloomed in impossible patterns, their leaves whispering secrets to the gentle breeze. Waterfalls cascaded from moss-covered rocks, their spray catching the light and creating miniature rainbows. Strange, glowing plants pulsed gently, illuminating hidden paths and secluded groves.

The air thrummed with a palpable sense of magic, a feeling that tickled Yuna's skin and made the hairs on her arms stand on end. It was a stark contrast to the mundane world she had left behind, a world where magic was only found in old books and whispered tales. Here, it was the very lifeblood of everything. With a mix of exhilaration and trepidation, Yuna stepped out of the carriage. The ground felt solid beneath her worn boots, a welcome sensation after hours of travel. She was dressed in the plain, practical clothes she had always worn, a stark contrast to the vibrant robes and cloaks of the other students bustling about. Already, she could see a kaleidoscope of colors and styles:

rich velvets in emerald and sapphire, silks embroidered with silver thread, and even practical leathers adorned with intricate spellwork.

She tugged at the hem of her simple tunic, feeling a pang of self-consciousness. She knew, intellectually, that her clothing shouldn't matter, but the sheer opulence of the surroundings made her feel like a small, insignificant pebble on a vast, shimmering beach. Despite her discomfort, she couldn't help but be awestruck by the sheer grandeur of the place. This was it. This was Arcanum Academy.

A young boy with tousled auburn hair and a mischievous grin emerged from the carriage next to hers. He wore a cloak of dark blue, embroidered with silver stars, and carried a well-worn spellbook tucked under his arm. He gave her a friendly nod, his eyes sparkling with amusement.

"First time, eh?" he asked, his voice carrying a hint of a cheerful lilt. "Don't worry, everyone feels like a gnome staring up at a giant...well, a giant that's also a magical school, I suppose."

Yuna managed a small smile, feeling a fraction of her anxiety ease. "Yes. I'm Yuna."

"Kael," he replied, extending a hand. His grip was firm and warm. "Welcome to the grandest asylum of arcane arts this side of the Aetherial Gate." He winked, making Yuna giggle.

Their brief introduction was interrupted by a sharp, clear voice that carried over the hubbub of arriving students. "Students, if you please! Gather 'round!"

A woman stood before them, tall and imposing, with silver hair pulled back in a severe bun. Her robes were of a deep violet, almost black, and her piercing blue eyes seemed to see right through them. This was Professor Elara Thorne, the Headmistress's first lieutenant, and the designated welcoming committee. Her very presence commanded respect, and the gathered students quickly quieted down. "Welcome to Arcanum Academy. I am Professor Thorne, and I will be assisting you with your orientation today. You will be divided into groups, and we will begin the proper induction process. Follow me." With that, she turned and strode towards a large stone archway, her robes billowing behind her like a dark cloud. Yuna, Kael, and a gaggle of other students hurried to follow.

The archway led into a vast courtyard, the centerpiece of which was a magnificent fountain. Carved from a single block of white marble, it depicted a dragon coiled around a tree, its wings spread in eternal flight. The water that flowed from the dragon's mouth shimmered with an iridescent light, and the air around it smelled of fresh herbs and ozone.

Professor Thorne paused, her eyes scanning the crowd. "I will now call out your names, and you will join your designated group. Please listen carefully." She unfurled a long scroll and began to read in a voice that was both commanding and resonant. As the names were called, the students shuffled into smaller circles, their nervous chatter slowly morphing into excited conversations. Yuna's heart pounded in her chest as she waited for her name to be called. She had no idea what to expect, not knowing anyone, and feeling very isolated. She didn't even know who to talk to and hoped to be placed with at least one friendly face. Would she fit in here? Would she be able to keep up with the other students, all of whom seemed so much more confident and assured than she felt?

Finally, her name was called. "Yuna Celestia! Group Three."

Yuna took a deep breath and stepped forward, her eyes scanning the crowd for her group. She spotted Kael, who gave her a small wave, and she quickly made her way towards him, feeling a sense of relief at seeing at least one familiar face. There were about eight other students gathered there, their faces a mixture of excitement and apprehension. Professor Thorne clapped her hands together, the sound echoing in the courtyard. "Group Three, you will be escorted by Ms. Willowbrook. Please follow her."

A young girl with long, flowing blonde hair and a kind smile stepped forward. She wore robes of a soft green, adorned with delicate embroidery of vines and leaves. She radiated a quiet confidence that immediately put Yuna at ease. "Greetings, everyone," she said, her voice warm and melodious. "I am Ms. Willowbrook, and it's my pleasure to welcome you to Arcanum. You are all very lucky to be here, and I'm excited for the adventure ahead of us. Please, follow me; we have much to see."

She turned and began to walk toward a narrow, stone pathway that wound through the enchanted gardens. Yuna and the rest of Group Three fell into step behind her, their initial nervousness slowly giving way to a sense of wonder. As they strolled through the gardens, Ms. Willowbrook began to share stories about the academy.

"Arcanum Academy has been a beacon of magical learning for centuries," she explained, her voice soft but clear. "It was founded by the esteemed wizard, Eldrin Arcanus, who believed that magic was a gift that should be nurtured and understood. The Academy is divided into five branches, each representing a different aspect of magical practice."

"Branches?" Kael asked, his brow furrowing. "Like some sort of...sorting?"

Ms. Willowbrook chuckled. "You've heard of the old tales, I see. Yes, in a sense. Each student is placed into a house based on their aptitude and affinities. The Branches are: Aetherius, which focuses on elemental magic; Lumina, which is dedicated to healing and light magic; Umbra, the house of shadow magic and illusions; Chronus, which is the house of time magic; and finally, Arcana, which delves into the study of all branches of magic. You will be given a series of tests over the next few days to determine which house is the best fit for you."

Yuna listened intently, her mind racing with possibilities. She had, until recently, never thought of what sort of magic was best for her. Her powers had come unbidden, and she had not thought about what they were or what their purpose was. It was simply magic, and she had accepted it. Now, the idea of different houses and different types of magic was fascinating. She wondered where she would ultimately end up.

As they walked deeper into the gardens, the path began to twist and turn, leading them through a series of hidden grottos and enchanting vistas. Yuna couldn't help but marvel at the beauty and complexity of the magical landscape, filled with strange and marvelous creatures and plants. She saw small, winged sprites flitting between the blooms, their bodies shimmering with iridescent light, and heard the gentle gurgle of fountains that seemed to hum with a soft, magical melody.

Ms. Willowbrook pointed out various plants and their magical properties, explaining how some could be used for healing, others for protection, and still others for more... esoteric... purposes. She even showed them a patch of moon petal flowers, their white petals glowing softly in the shade. "These bloom only under the light of the full moon," she explained, her voice filled with a sense of reverence. "And their nectar can grant temporary visions of the future."

The other students in the group, caught up in the wonder of the gardens, asked questions eagerly, their initial nervousness forgotten in the awe of their new surroundings. Yuna was quiet, taking it all in, too mesmerized by everything around her to form questions. Her head was swimming with the sheer volume of knowledge being thrown at her. She had never witnessed magic like this before, and all she could do was gape at every new thing, trying to absorb it all.

They finally reached the end of their garden tour and stepped out into another courtyard, this one much smaller and more intimate than the one they had entered upon their arrival. In the center of the courtyard stood a tall oak tree, its branches reaching towards the sky like gnarled fingers. A small, wooden door was nestled into the base of the tree.

"This is the entrance to the student dormitories," Ms. Willowbrook announced, her voice laced with a note of finality. "We have reached the end of your orientation tour today. The door will lead you to the reception hall of the main dorm. There will be house guides to help you with your respective room assignments. You will find a schedule of the coming days in your rooms. Please enjoy yourselves, and don't hesitate to seek help if needed." She smiled warmly and bowed her head, before quickly walking away. The students remained a moment, blinking at the tree door. Yuna felt a renewed wave of anxiety washed over her. This was it. She was officially on her own, and the reality of that both excited and terrified her. The others seemed to feel similarly, and their initial energy had worn off, replaced once again by apprehension and uncertainty. For a moment, no one moved, each of them contemplating the unknown that lay just beyond the small wooden door.

Kael, ever the optimist, broke the silence. "Well, what are we waiting for?" he said, a grin spreading across his face. "Let's go see what awaits us on the other side!"

With a deep breath, Yuna followed him and the others as they stepped through the door.

The door opened into a spacious hall, dimly lit by glowing crystals embedded into the walls. The air here was calm and still, a stark contrast to the vibrant energy of the gardens. Long wooden tables were arranged along the length of the hall, with house guides seated at each one. They nodded at the arriving students, some smiling welcomingly, others looking more reserved. Yuna and the others clustered nervously together, trying to figure out where they belonged.

A young woman with dark braided hair and piercing green eyes stood up from one of the tables. She wore robes of a deep blue engraved with a koala, easily identifying her as a guide for the House of Lumina. "Welcome to the dormitories," she said, her voice clear and calm. "Please find the table that corresponds to your assigned house. If you are not sure which branch you belong to, come to me for assistance."

The students exchanged nervous glances, unsure of where to go. Yuna suddenly felt lost again, the sheer size of the hall and the number of people made her feel overwhelmed. She wished she had a better idea of what to expect. Her head was still reeling from the tour, and now she was facing yet another new experience that was making her stomach drop.

Kael, sensing her discomfort, nudged her gently. "Come on," he said, his voice reassuring. "Let's figure this out together."

Together, they approached the guides. Yuna suddenly realized that most students seemed to have predetermined affiliations, their outfits giving them away, but she had no idea how or why. It seemed like there was a lot that she simply did not know. They approached the guide with dark braids, explaining that they were not yet assigned, and she pointed them both to a far table. There, at one end, sat a young boy with dark, wavy hair, his robes a deep sapphire blue, embroidered with silver crescents. He looked up as the newcomers approached.

"Greetings, new students," he said, his voice soft and welcoming. "I am Silas, a guide for the House of Arcana. The non-affiliated are sent to me by default. Please, take a seat."

Yuna and Kael hesitantly took seats along the table, quickly noticing that most of the students there seemed just as lost and confused as they were. Silas started to speak, his voice calming everyone.

"As Ms. Willowbrook told you, you will be tested over the next few days to determine your house alignment. In the meantime, you will be residing in the Undesignated Quarters. They are not part of a specific house, but very comfortable. You will be provided with a map of the academy, your schedules, and a list of resources that you may need." He started shuffling through a pile of papers, pulling one out each time he finished speaking.

"Yuna Celestia?"

Yuna jumped a little, startled by the sound of her name. "Here," she replied, taking the proffered envelope along with a thin map.

"Kael Stencia?"

"That's me!" Kael replied, taking his things with a smile.

Silas continued to call names and distribute the items until everyone at the table had been helped. "Please check the map, and you should find directions to the Undesignated Quarters," he said. "You are free to explore the academy if you wish, but just ensure that nothing is touched or altered without permission. The rules of the Academy are in your envelope, and we expect them to be followed. And finally, please rest."

Yuna opened her envelope, her hands still shaking slightly. Inside, she found a small, intricate map of the academy grounds, more detailed than she had imagined. The schedule was a simple list, detailing the various tests they would be taking over the next few days, with a time for each one. The rules seemed rather daunting, but as she scanned them, they didn't seem all that onerous. She noted with a little sigh that there was also a list of prohibited items, which included several mundane items that she had completely overlooked, as well as a list of forbidden spells. She suddenly felt rather unprepared.

Kael leaned over, looking at her schedule with interest. "Looks like they're putting us right to work," he said with a grin. "I'm actually kind of excited." Yuna couldn't muster quite as much enthusiasm. She felt a strange sense of trepidation, a nagging feeling that she was not ready for what lay ahead. Still, she appreciated Kael's optimism.

They followed the directions on the map, weaving through a maze of corridors and staircases, until they finally reached the Undesignated Quarters. It was a small, self-contained wing of the academy, with a series of simple but comfortable rooms arranged along a central corridor. Each room had its bed, a small desk, and a wardrobe. The décor was neutral and calming, designed to be suitable for all students, regardless of their house alignment.

Yuna stepped into her room, feeling a mix of relief and weariness. She placed her belongings on the bed, the simple act of unpacking a few things giving her a sliver of normalcy. She sat down for a moment, staring at the ceiling, trying to process the whirlwind of the last few hours. She had arrived at a magical academy, a place she had only dreamed about, and yet, she felt more lost and confused than ever. Was she even ready for this? She wanted to call out to her Grandma, to get some comfort, but she knew that was not possible. She had decided to leave, and she knew that this change had to be for the better. She shook her head. She was here now. She had to make the best of it.

With a sigh, she opened the Academy Rules and began to read. It seemed to be mostly common sense things but also stated several consequences for rule-breaking that seemed rather strict. She quickly read the list, trying to parse as much of it as possible before beginning her new life here. She quickly changed into comfortable nightclothes, exhausted from the day, and stretched out on the bed.

As she drifted off to sleep, Yuna couldn't help but wonder what the next few days would bring. Would she find her place at Arcanum Academy? Would she ever feel like she belonged? And what secrets lay hidden beneath the surface of this magical place? Only time, it seemed, would tell. The next morning, Yuna woke with a start, disoriented for a moment before remembering where she was. The room was bathed in the soft light of early morning, the sun streaming through the tall windows. She sat up in bed, stretching her stiff limbs, and then glanced at the schedule that was still lying on her desk. It was time to start her testing. She dressed quickly, putting on the same clothes as the day before. She noticed with some discomfort that none of the students in Arcanum were wearing their day-to-day clothing, and she once again felt out of place. She tried to ignore the thought, and instead reminded herself that it didn't matter what she had on. It was what she did with her time here that counted. She decided to go find Kael before she started her day. She opened her door and slipped out into the corridor, noticing that some other students were milling about, all of whom seemed just as groggy as she did. She saw him standing near the common area and headed his way.

"Good morning, sleepyhead," Kael said with a chuckle, noticing her approach. "Ready to tackle this first day of testing?"

Yuna nodded, trying to force a smile. "I guess so. Nervous, though, I have to admit."

"I know the feeling," he said, "But I believe we're going to do great. All we have to do is be ourselves and do our best." He shrugged as if it was the easiest thing in the world.

Together, they made their way to the main hall, where they had been told to gather for the first round of testing. The room was already filled with students, a mix of nervous chatter and anxious energy. Professor Thorne stood at the front, her presence just as commanding as it had been the day before. "Students," she said, her voice crisp and clear, "Today begins the first round of aptitude testing. You will be called up one by one to complete a series of basic exercises designed to gauge your natural magical inclinations. Please remain calm and follow the instructions that will be given to you." Yuna's heart began to pound in her chest. She had no idea what to expect. Was she even going to be capable of anything? She had no real concept of her capabilities and felt a cold fear creeping up her spine. She just wanted to pass here; she wanted to gain some sort of understanding of her abilities and herself.

The first test was a simple one, designed to gauge their elemental affinities. Each student was given a small stone and asked to focus their magic on it, trying to alter its composition based on the element they felt most connected to. As the students stepped forward, one by one, Yuna observed, trying to learn from their experience. Some were able to heat the stone until it glowed red, others to cool it until it frosted over. One student even managed to manipulate the stone itself, causing it to shift into a different shape before being quickly called off by one of the instructors. When it was finally her turn, Yuna stepped forward, her hands trembling slightly. She took the stone in her hands, closing her eyes. She tried to focus, to feel the connection she was supposed to be experiencing. It was difficult, like trying to grasp at a wisp of smoke. She simply felt the stone in her hands, cold, inert. She tried again, using all of her concentration. She visualized fire and heat. She didn't know what she was supposed to do, or how she was even supposed to understand what to visualize.

However, despite her lack of visualization, something was happening. Yuna opened her eyes, surprised to see the stone in her hand glowing with a flame, It was fire, particularly elemental. It was simply a soft, glowing light. It felt strange to her, something she hadn't experienced before. The instructor, a stern-looking woman with a high, pointed hat, raised an eyebrow at her she said. " An elemental affinity." She jotted something down on a clipboard, not offering any further explanation. Yuna was left feeling confused and even more uncertain than before. She was an anomaly of some kind. She found Kael in the crowd of students and walked over to sit next to him.

"How did it go?" Kael asked, his eyes full of curiosity.

Yuna shook her head with a mixture of feelings. "mine turned to fire! Kael. I didn't feel anything The instructor said I did have an elemental affinity."

Kael jumped with happiness. "Well, that's great. I made mine turn to wind. We'd be in the same house, so we could hang out!"

"I know, it would be fun," Yuna said, feeling motivated.

She tried her best, focusing on the words given by the instructors, but each time she was left feeling more and more confused. She had no idea what her magic was capable of or how it was supposed to work.

CHAPTER III

Secrets of the Arcanum

The initial buzz of arrival at the Arcanum had begun to settle, replaced by the structured rhythm of classes. Yuna, however, found her attention constantly drifting. The lectures on basic enchanting and potion brewing, while informative, felt like a surface skim compared to the depths she yearned to explore. While her peers diligently copied notes and practiced wand movements, Yuna felt an almost magnetic pull toward the Arcanum's library. It wasn't just the allure of books; it was something more, a whisper in the back of her mind, a feeling of a hidden path waiting to be uncovered.

The Arcanum's library was not merely a collection of texts; it was a labyrinth of knowledge, a towering structure of stone and timber, its countless shelves reaching towards the vaulted ceiling like the branches of a petrified forest. The air hung thick with the scent of aged parchment, binding glue, and the faintest hint of dust, a perfume both comforting and intoxicating to Yuna. Sunlight streamed through the tall arched windows, illuminating motes of dust dancing in the air like tiny, ephemeral spirits. It was a place where time seemed to slow, where the hushed rustling of turning pages replaced the clamor of the outside world.

Unlike many of her classmates who favored the more well-trodden paths of spellcraft, Yuna found herself drawn to the library's less frequented sections. She'd wander past the brightly lit areas dedicated to current magical theory and contemporary spellbooks, her feet leading her deeper into the shadows. It was in these neglected corners, amongst shelves laden with forgotten lore and bound in cracked leather, that she began her true education. One afternoon, after a particularly frustrating lesson on summoning minor imps (hers kept turning into disgruntled squirrels), Yuna made her way to her usual haven. She bypassed the bustling main hall of the library and slipped through a narrow archway leading to a section labeled "Eldorian History – Archaic Texts." The lighting here was dim, the long, narrow aisles bordered by towering shelves that seemed to press close, holding secrets silently.

She ran a hand along the spines of the books, her fingertips tracing the worn gold lettering. The titles, mostly in Old Eldorian, were cryptic, hinting at ages long past. 'The Echoes of the First Mages,' one read. 'Chronicles of the Shadow Wars,' proclaimed another. There were books bound in heavy wood, sealed with tarnished clasps, and others so fragile they seemed to crumble at a mere touch.

Yuna pulled a particularly thick volume from a shelf. It was bound in dark, almost black leather, its cover embossed with an intricate symbol – a circle surrounding a three-pointed star, the points extending outwards like stylized flames. The lettering on the spine was almost completely faded, but she could just make out the faint traces of 'Guardians of Eldoria.'

Her heart quickened. It was unlike any book she had seen before, and an inexplicable sense of urgency propelled her forward. She found a small, dusty table tucked away in a corner and settled down, carefully opening the book.

The pages were brittle, the ink faded in places. It was written in a mixture of Old Eldorian and a script she had only ever seen referenced in passing in her basic magical history class – a language known as the 'Runes of the Ancient Wardens'. Yuna spent a long moment deciphering the first few passages, her brow furrowed in concentration.

The text spoke of a time before the current age, a period when Eldoria wasn't just a land, but a vibrant nexus of magical energy, a place where the veil between the realms was thin. It described a group of individuals, not just mages, but beings who held a deep connection to the land itself. These were the Guardians, protectors of Eldoria, those who stood against the encroaching darkness. They were not just warriors wielding spells; they were also keepers of ancient knowledge, weavers of the very magic that sustained the realm.

As she delved deeper, she realized that these Guardians weren't just historical figures, they were a lineage, a family of protectors that had existed for generations, each one passing down their knowledge and power to the next. Her breath hitched.

The book detailed the Guardians' responsibilities, their methods, and their most well-guarded secret - the existence of the 'Arcanum' itself, not just the place she was sitting in, but the source from which all magic flowed. She had been taught that magic was a gift from the land, a natural force, but this book spoke of it as a conscious entity, a wellspring of power, protected by the Guardians.

Yuna's fingers trembled as she turned the page. There, amidst the faded ink and intricate illustrations of ancient magical artifacts, she saw a family tree. It wasn't a simple list of names; it was a tangled web of connections, of bloodlines interwoven with the very fabric of Eldoria. And as she followed the lines backward in time, her eyes widened.

She saw name after name, each one linked to a symbol, each one associated with a description of immense power and unwavering dedication. And then, her gaze landed on a branch closer to the top.

There, amidst the fading ink, was a name – "Anya of the Whispering Woods." Underneath, it showed her symbol - a stylized depiction of a silver crescent moon cradled by oak leaves. And bbesidesthat name, smaller, more faded, but undeniably there, was her family name – "Everwood."

Yuna's heart pounded in her chest. Her family? Guardians of Eldoria? She had grown up in the heart of the Whispering Woods, a place she had always felt deeply connected to, yet she had never heard stories like this. Her parents had spoken of the old ways, of respecting the land, but never of a lineage of Guardians.

A wave of dizziness washed over her. She leaned back in her chair, the book sliding from her grasp to the table with a soft thud. Could this be real? Could her family, the family of quiet woodsmen and herbalists she'd known all her life, be connected to such a powerful and ancient heritage? She reached out and touched the symbol of the silver moon and oak leaves, the same symbol she had seen in her mother's worn silver locket, which she'd always thought was just an old family heirloom. Her mother had always worn it, never taking it off, saying it was a 'reminder of who we are'.

A thousand questions filled her mind, all swirling together in a chaotic torrent of uncertainty. Why had her parents never told her? Were they hiding something? Or did they not even know? If that were true, it implied that the knowledge had been lost, hidden away, perhaps even deliberately forgotten.

She spent the rest of the afternoon lost in the book, meticulously deciphering passages, her small candle casting long flickering shadows on the tall shelves. She learned of the great Shadow Wars, of the terrible battles fought against creatures of darkness that threatened to consume Eldoria. She discovered the rituals of the Guardians, their connection to the four elements, and the ancient magic they wielded to protect their land. She learned about the 'Wellspring of Knowledge'— the source of the Arcanum's power — and its delicate balance and protection by the Guardians. If that power ever falls into the wrong hands, the consequences could be catastrophic.

The sun had long since set, the library's windows turning into dark, blank squares against the deepening twilight. The only light came from her candle and the faint glow of the enchanted orbs that dotted the library ceiling. It was after hours, and the library staff would soon be making their rounds, closing up for the night. Yuna knew she couldn't stay, not here, not yet. She carefully marked her place in the book, tucking a small flower petal between the pages, and placed the ancient tome back on the shelf. She slipped out, her mind a whirlwind of niscoveries and unanswered questions.

That night in her dormitory, Yuna couldn't sleep. The image of the family tree, the symbol of the silver moon and oak leaves, kept flashing behind her eyes. The world she had known, her understanding of her family and her place in it, had been irrevocably altered. She could no longer look at the Arcanum, or Eldoria itself, in the same way. She had found a secret, and it was calling to her, demanding to be explored.

The next day, instead of attending her enchanting class, Yuna returned to the library. This time she went straight to the section on Archaic Texts, bypassing the more popular areas, her steps purposeful. She wanted more than just information, she needed confirmation. She pulled another book from the shelves, a smaller, thinner volume titled 'The Lineage of the Guardians'. This one contained more detailed information about the individual Guardians, their unique powers, and their personalities. As she flipped through the pages, she found it. The name "Anya of the Whispering Woods" again, this time with a more extensive description: 'A Guardian of unparalleled connection to nature, able to communicate with flora and fauna, and wield the magic of the wild.' It described her as fiercely protective, exceptionally wise, and a master of healing magic.

There was also mention of "Aakari", Anya's descendant from a time closer to the current era. The text described him as a 'powerful mage, but one who chose seclusion' and 'focused on preserving the ancient knowledge, rather than using it in open conflict'. He was noted as being the Guardian who began to record the secrets of the lineage in coded texts and hidden locations. This information resonated with Yuna's experience, explaining why the knowledge had been hidden. As she continued her reading, Yuna came across a passage that made her heart leap. The Guardians, the text explained, weren't just protectors, they were also chosen by the Arcanum itself. Each Guardian was born with a unique 'resonance' to the magic of the land, a predisposition to certain abilities, and a deep connection to the Wellspring. The Arcanum actively sought out those who possessed this resonance, and their birth was always marked by specific signs or occurrences within the land.

A memory flashed before her eyes – a vivid recollection from her childhood. She recalled the night she was born, a night the Whispering Woods had come alive with a strange, luminescent glow that her older sister, Elara, had described as 'the trees whispering secrets to the stars'. At the time, it had seemed like a fantastical tale; now, it held a deeper, more significant meaning. This was why she felt drawn to the library, why the magic of Eldoria felt so familiar, so intrinsically part of her. She might not have known of her heritage, but the Arcanum knew her. She wasn't just a student, she was a descendant of the Guardians, and the Arcanum was whispering her name.

For days, Yuna immersed herself in the library, her studies taking a backseat to her exploration of her family's secrets. She learned to decipher the Runes of the Ancient Wardens, navigate the archaic language, and understand the subtle nuances of ancient magic. She neglected her meals; sleep was a luxury she could barely afford. She was driven by a relentless need to know more, to uncover every hidden detail of her lineage.

She discovered that the Guardians did not only protect the realm from physical threats but also served as wardens of the Arcanum, guardians of the magical balance. Their duty was not only to wield power but also to understand its intricacies, to prevent it from being misused. It was a responsibility that extended through generations, passed down from elder to younger, from parent to child. The weight of it settled on Yuna's shoulders, a heavy cloak of destiny that both excited and frightened her. She also learned of the 'Shadow Stones', ancient artifacts imbued with dark energy, and how they were used against the Guardians during the Shadow Wars. The Guardians had managed to contain them, to prevent their power from being unleashed, but the texts warned that they could not be destroyed, only hidden. She found fragmented maps that pointed toward the rumored locations of these stones, and a chilling depiction of a ritual designed to unlock their power.

As she explored further, she found small, coded passages within some of the books, notes written in a script that was not immediately apparent. It was an intricate form of writing, utilizing not just words, but symbols and images to convey its meaning. It took hours of painstaking effort, carefully cross-referencing different texts and deciphering fragments before she finally began to understand it. The passages appeared to be personal journal entries, written by various Guardians over the centuries. They contained their thoughts, their fears, and their hopes for the future, as well as detailed information on their inners, the rituals they performed, and the locations of hidden magical sites across Eldoria. There was an underlying tone of warning in most of them, a constant reminder of the responsibility they carried and the threat that still lurked in the shadows.

Among these journal entries, Yuna found one that particularly captured her attention. It was written by her ancestor, Aakari, the Guardian mentioned as the one who began the coded texts. The entry spoke about the need to prepare for a 'coming storm', a darkness that would one day threaten to engulf Eldoria once again. Elias had written that only those 'who carry the blood of the Guardians, and the resilience of the woods' would be able to withstand the darkness when it returned.

He also mentioned a 'hidden chamber' within the Arcanum itself, a place where the most ancient artifacts and knowledge of the Guardians were kept, a passage that was only accessible to those who possessed the true 'resonance.' He had described a test, a series of trials designed to assess the strength of a Guardian's connection to the Arcanum and their power, and the chamber would reveal itself only to one who truly deserved the title of Guardian. Yuna felt a shiver of anticipation run down her spine. It was becoming increasingly clear that her discovery was not a coincidence. The Arcanum had guided her, drawn her to the right books, the right hidden passages. She was not just uncovering her family's past; she was being prepared for a future that was both terrifying and exhilarating.

She was so engrossed in her research that she was barely aware of the passage of time. Days blurred into nights, and the library became her entire world. She found herself thinking like a Guardian too, her mind constantly focused on understanding the magic and the responsibility she had to her lineage. The other students at the Arcanum became distant figures, their concerns trivial compared to the weight of her discoveries. She still went to classes, though her mind was often far from the professor's lectures. She practiced her spells, though her heart was always set on the secrets of the ancient texts.

One evening, as she was poring over a particularly cryptic passage, she noticed a symbol etched into the corner of the page – a stylized depiction of a twisting, thorny vine. The same symbol that adorned her family's old walking stick, the one that had been passed down through generations. She had always thought it was just an aesthetic detail, never realizing it held a deeper meaning. With renewed determination, she began searching for other books mentioning the vine symbol. She found references in texts about the nature of the Whispering Woods, about the deep magic that flowed through its very roots. It was described as a 'living map' created by the Guardians, a series of hidden pathways and magical markers etched into the trees and the undergrowth. It was a way to navigate the forest safely and a way to hide secrets from those who were not meant to find them. Her mind raced, pieces falling into place like the turning of a complex lock. The Whispering Woods was not just a place, it was a living archive, a repository of the Guardians' ancient knowledge, carefully guarded by the magic of the vines. She wondered about the hidden pathways it might contain, about the secrets her parents might have been protecting.

Yuna had spent nearly two weeks now in the depths of the library, the constant pursuit of knowledge keeping her driven.

She had become completely absorbed in her research and had lost her awareness of the day-to-day activities of the Arcanum.

One morning, however, as she was making her way through the library, she saw a notice posted on the bulletin board. She paused to read it, her eyes widened in surprise. She had almost forgotten about it, but the notice was a reminder of the upcoming 'Inter-Arcanum Tournament', a competition between magical schools across Eldoria. The tournament was a tradition, a test of skills, and a celebration of magical prowess. Every Arcanum was expected to send their most talented students to compete in various challenges, ranging from duels and spell casting to potion making and magical theory. It was a prestigious event, and the winner would bring great honor to their respective school.

Yuna had heard whispers about the tournament, but she had been so engrossed in her discoveries that she hadn't given it much thought. But the notice on the board made her realize that the tournament was not just a competition; it was also a gathering of powerful mages from all over Eldoria. It was an opportunity to learn more about the current state of magic, about the threats her ancestors had faced, and potentially to find others who possessed a similar understanding of the ancient ways. A sense of urgency washed over her. Despite her passion for uncovering the secrets of the past, she realized she couldn't neglect the present. She had to master her magic, hone her skills, and prepare for the challenges that lay ahead, not just as a student of the Arcanum, but also as a potential Guardian. She knew she couldn't do it alone. She needed guidance, someone with whom she could share her discoveries, someone to help her navigate the complex web of magic and responsibility. She considered talking to Professor Eldrin, the headmaster, but she wasn't sure if she could trust him with the secret of her lineage. She needed someone who would understand the weight of her burden, someone who might share her connection to the ancient ways. She thought about Elara, her sister, who had always been attuned to the whispers of the woods. She thought of her mother, with her silver locket and her cryptic warnings, her father who always had an inherent respect for nature that went beyond what Yuna had ever experienced. She felt a sudden longing for her family, a deep desire for connection and for guidance she so yearned for. She spent the rest of that day going over a passage she had discovered about the Guardians' training, focusing on the importance of meditation and connection to nature. The texts spoke of a ritual known as 'The Whispering Breath', a meditative technique designed to awaken a Guardian's innate power and strengthen their connection to the Arcanum. She felt that the method was calling to her, guiding her on the path she needed to take.

That night, instead of returning to the library, Yuna sought out a quiet corner of the Arcanum's inner gardens. The moon was high in the sky, bathing the ancient trees and hedges in a soft silver light. She sat on the grass beneath an ancient willow, her back against its trunk, and closed her eyes. She took a deep breath, letting the cool night air fill her lungs, and focused her mind on the rhythm of her heartbeat. The sounds of the night, the rustling of leaves, and the chirping of insects, slowly receded into the background.

She imagined herself as a tree, her roots burrowing deep into the earth, drawing energy from the very core of Eldoria. She felt herself becoming one with the land, with the magic that flowed through its veins. She repeated the ancient mantra she had learned from the texts, a simple phrase that spoke of balance and harmony. She felt a subtle tingling sensation begin in her fingers, a warmth spreading through her chest, and a deeper sense of peace settled within her. She could feel the magic of the Arcanum flowing through her, a cool, vibrant energy that both soothed and empowered her.

She practiced for what felt like hours, her mind clear, her body relaxed, and her connection to the land grew stronger with each passing moment. She felt the presence of the Arcanum, a conscious hum of energy, acknowledging her, welcoming her.

She understood that she wasn't just a student at the Arcanum, she was a part of it, an extension of its magic. She also realized that her training could not end here, she needed to return to the forest, to the Whispering Woods that held so many secrets for her to uncover. But she couldn't leave just yet, more preparation here would be invaluable.

When she finally opened her eyes, the first rays of dawn were beginning to paint the sky with hues of pink and gold. She felt invigorated, her mind clearer, her sense of purpose solidified. She knew what she had to do. She had to embrace her heritage, hone her skills, and prepare for the challenges ahead. The discovery of her lineage had awakened something within her, a dormant power that she was only just beginning to understand. She was not just Yuna Everwood, the student; she was Yuna Everwood, the descendant of the Guardians, the protector of Eldoria. She carried a heavy responsibility, but she was no longer alone. She had her family, her past, and her destiny, to guide her on the path she had been chosen to walk.

The Arcanum wasn't just a school for her now, it was the heart of her heritage, a place to hone her powers in preparation for the road ahead, the road that would inevitably be fraught with danger. As Yuna began to attend her classes once more, she carried a new sense of purpose and determination. She studied with a new focus, her mind fully engaged in the lessons, making connections that she had not previously considered. She also sought opportunities to practice her spells, not just in the classroom, but also in the gardens and training grounds of the Arcanum. She paid close attention to her professors' advice, carefully incorporating their teachings into her practice.

She discovered that her connection to nature made her particularly adept at plant-based magic and healing spells. When other students struggled with a particularly challenging incantation, she found that the words flowed freely from her tongue. When others fumbled with a potion, she knew instinctively the right amount of herbs to use. She realized she possessed an understanding of the natural world that went beyond mere book learning. These were not mere talents, but echoes of her Guardian ancestors, their powers flowing through her. She began to spend her evenings in the library, but now, instead of just focusing on her family's past, she also began to study more current magical disciplines, particularly those that related to combat and defense. She realized that she had to be a warrior as well as a scholar if she wanted to protect Eldoria from the darkness. She needed to protect the power of the Arcanum, the power that guided her, and the land she loved.

She knew that the tournament was fast approaching, and she would need to be at her best if she wanted to make her presence felt. But more importantly, she understood the importance of the event, a gathering of powerful mages from all over Eldoria, and a chance to learn more about the challenges she might soon have to face. It was more than a competition; it was a prelude to something greater. A trial by fire, perhaps.

But she felt prepared now, her training underway, her destiny becoming more apparent with every passing day.

CHAPTER IV

Fractured Friendships

The air in the Grand Hall of Aethelgard crackled, not with elemental magic, but with the barely contained energy of a new school year. Yuna, perched on the edge of a long oak table, swung her legs, her bright emerald eyes darting around the hall, absorbing the vibrant chaos. The morning sun, streaming through the arched windows, caught the glint of gold in her braided hair, turning it into a halo of light. Her enthusiasm, as always, was a tangible thing, a whirlwind of motion and buoyant laughter that often left a trail of startled smiles or, conversely, irritated glares in its wake.

"Did you see that golem, Elara? The one near the east gate? It's massive! I bet it could hurl those practice dummies clear over the training field!" Yuna exclaimed, her voice carrying across the table to her friend, Elara, who meticulously stacked a pyramid of sugar cubes. Elara, ever the picture of calm, blinked slowly, her long, dark eyelashes fluttering against her cheek.

"Yuna, you'd be impressed by a particularly well-placed pebble. It's just a golem. They're designed for that purpose." Elara's voice was soft, a quiet counterpoint to Yuna's effervescence. She adjusted her spectacles, her gaze never wavering from the meticulous task at hand. Yuna laughed, a bright, bell-like sound. "Oh, you're no fun, Elara! Where's your adventurous spirit? What if that golem wasn't guarding the gate? What if it was a rebel golem? A golem on a quest for...for...sugar cubes!" Elara finally allowed a small smile to touch her lips. "Then I fear I'd be its first target." She carefully placed the final cube on the top of her pyramid, a perfect, gleaming structure.

This playful banter was typical of their friendship. Yuna, the whirlwind of energy and impulsiveness, and Elara, the quiet observer, the meticulous planner. They were different as night and day, yet their connection was a solid, comforting presence in the sometimes tumultuous world of Aethelgard.

As Yuna continued to chatter about the possibilities of rebellious golems, her gaze was drawn to a figure entering the hall. Callum. He moved with a casual grace, a languid charm that seemed almost effortless. His dark hair was slightly tousled, as if he had just emerged from a particularly intense dream, and his eyes, a deep, intriguing blue, seemed to hold secrets that he was reluctant to share. He possessed an innate charisma that drew attention effortlessly. Callum caught Yuna's eye, a faint smile curving his lips, and dipped his head in a silent greeting. Yuna felt a familiar flutter in her chest, a warmth spreading through her, though she would have vehemently denied that it was anything more than friendly acknowledgment. She waved back, a little too enthusiastically, almost knocking over a pitcher of water.

"Who was that?" Elara asked, finally looking up from her sugar cube masterpiece.

"That's Callum," Yuna replied, her voice a little too casual, her eyes still following Callum as he made his way to a table near the windows. "He's in our year. I think...I think he's quite interesting."

Elara raised a skeptical eyebrow, not quite meeting Yuna's gaze, clearly sensing that "interesting" had a deeper meaning. "Interesting how?" she asked, knowing how Yuna tended to gravitate towards puzzles.

Yuna shrugged, trying to feign disinterest. "Just...interesting. He's very quiet, and seems like he is always thinking. Like he knows things everyone else doesn't."

Elara hummed, skeptical. "Everyone thinks they 'know things others don't.' It's rarely true."

Meanwhile, as Yuna was trying to feign disinterest, Callum was the subject of a different sort of attention at the window table. Maris, her dark hair pulled back in a severe bun, watched him with a calculating gaze. She was a picture of composed elegance, sharp edges and controlled movements, and her elemental power could be felt even in her stillness. She was gifted with the control of earth and water, a powerful and rare combination. She didn't smile, and it always seemed like she was looking for a challenge. "He's putting on an act," Maris said, her voice as sharp as chipped flint. She hadn't looked directly at him, but Callum knew she was talking about him. "That 'mysterious charm' routine. It's pathetic."

Her friend Bren, a burly boy with a shock of untamed red hair, chuckled. "Someone's jealous."

Maris shot him a glare that could have frozen lava. "Jealous? Of him? Don't be ridiculous, Bren. I simply dislike pretension."

"I think he's alright," another student at their table, a girl called Orla, added quietly. Orla had a gift with plants and herbs, and her gentle nature often put her at odds with Maris's sharper attitudes. "He seems... thoughtful."

Maris snorted, the sound cutting through the air like a snapped twig. "Thoughtful? You're mistaking his aloofness for something profound. He's probably thinking of how best to manipulate people."

"You assume the worst of everyone," Bren observed.

"Because most people are," Maris countered, her eyes flashing. "And Callum is one of them. He's far too... smooth."

Callum, despite his efforts to appear detached, heard their conversation. He didn't react outwardly, but a subtle tension tightened the muscles in his jaw. He knew that Maris was watching him, analyzing him, and her animosity was as clear as the bell chimes that marked the beginning of classes. As the hall started to fill with more eager students, Yuna was still watching Callum, her thoughts whirling. She had only exchanged a few words with him since the start of the year, but he was a magnetic presence, a riddle that she longed to unravel. His air of quiet confidence was intriguing, and in a way, it pulled her towards him, even though she knew she should probably focus on her studies.

"Yuna," Elara said, her voice sharper than usual, breaking through Yuna's reverie. "Are you even listening to me?"

Yuna blinked, turning her attention back to her friend. "Sorry, Elara. What were you saying?"

Elara sighed, a small puff of air that ruffled her bangs. "I was saying that Professor Theron's first alchemy lesson is notoriously difficult. You need to focus if you want to pass. Staring at Callum across the room will not help your results." Yuna flushed slightly, a telltale sign of her being caught in a wandering thought. "I wasn't staring," she mumbled, but her voice lacked conviction.

Elara simply raised an eyebrow, a silent commentary on Yuna's flimsy denial. "Just focus, Yuna. We have a difficult term ahead, and there are far more important things than boys with mysterious smiles." Yuna nodded, knowing that Elara was right. But even as she promised to concentrate, her eyes couldn't help but drift back to where Callum was sitting, a faint, almost subconscious tug pulling her in his direction.

The bell chimed, the sound echoing through the hall like a clarion call, signaling the start of classes. A flurry of movement rippled through the hall as students gathered their belongings and headed toward their designated classrooms. Yuna and Elara joined the flow, Elara walking with her usual measured pace, while Yuna weaved through the crowd with a restless energy, her gaze still occasionally seeking out Callum. The tension between those who admired and resented Yuna was becoming palpable.

The first few weeks of the new term were a whirlwind of lessons, practical training, and late-night study sessions. Yuna threw herself into her studies, her natural aptitude for magic shining through in her spells and incantations. She excelled in Potions, her hands moving with a natural dexterity, her keen eye for detail always ensuring the correct balance of ingredients. In Charms, she was a natural, her laughter often echoing through the classroom as she brought inanimate objects to life, her imagination knowing no bounds. But despite her academic success, Yuna found herself increasingly distracted by Callum.

In passing moments, a glimpse across the courtyard, a brief exchange in the library, An accidental brush of hands during practical, she found herself drawn further into his orbit.

She had managed to strike up a conversation with him on only a few occasions, always brief, filled with a polite, but slightly strained cordiality. He was reserved, and almost guarded, and his answers often left her with more questions than she had started with. She learned that he was adept at defense magic, but he often avoided any discussion of his past or his ambitions. There was a shadow behind his charm, a hint of sadness that she couldn't quite place.

During a joint transfiguration class, where they worked in pairs, Yuna and Callum were partnered together. The task was to transform a simple stone into a small, winged creature. Yuna's enthusiasm bubbled over as she and Callum carefully positioned their stones on the workbench between them.

"This will be fun, won't it?" Yuna asked, her eyes shining with anticipation. "What sort of creature do you think we should create? A raven? Or maybe a butterfly? Or something more... exotic?" She gestured with her hands, already conjuring fantastical images in her mind.

Callum watched her with a small, almost imperceptible smile. "Perhaps we should start with something simple. No need to jump straight into the fantastical." His tone was gentle, but it held an undercurrent of something unreadable.

Yuna nodded, her enthusiasm slightly dimmed by his practicality. "Okay, you're right. A simple, small bird then? Maybe a sparrow?"

They began the incantation, their voices blending together as they focused their magic on the stones. Yuna's magic flowed freely, her touch light and effortless, while Callum's was more measured, precise, every flicker of power controlled. The stone between them began to shift, to change, to reshape itself. The process was exhilarating, the combined magical energy creating a palpable buzz in the air around them. Their finished product was a small, brown robin, which fluttered to life before them.

"It's beautiful," Yuna breathed, watching the robin take flight and circle around their heads. "You're incredibly gifted, Callum."

Callum dipped his head, a faint color rising in his cheeks. "You are too, Yuna," he said softly. "Your magic is... bright."

"Bright?" Yuna tilted her head, a puzzled expression on her face. "What do you mean by bright?"

Callum hesitated for a moment, his eyes searching her face as though he was about to say something more profound, before a shift occurred and his usual guardedness dropped back into place. "It's... strong," he said, his tone shifting to more casual. "It's easy to see."

Before Yuna could press him further, Professor Blackwood, their transfiguration instructor, called for the class' attention. The lesson drew to a close, and Yuna found herself staring at Callum as he collected his belongings. She wanted to talk to him more, to understand the mystery that surrounded him, but she didn't have the courage to push too hard.

As she and Elara walked back to the dorms after class, Yuna tried to process the interaction, her mind full of Callum's words and movements.

"He called my magic 'bright,' Elara!" she said, her voice filled with a mixture of confusion and excitement. "I don't know what he meant by that, but it... it felt important."

Elara remained silent for a moment, then sighed. "Yuna, you're reading too much into things. Perhaps he simply meant your magic is potent. Stop obsessing over it."

Yuna frowned, her enthusiasm deflating. "But he looked like he was about to say something more! Like he was holding back."
"People hold back all the time Yuna," Elara said, her voice patient but firm. "Especially people you've just met. It doesn't mean there's a hidden message behind every interaction. It could just mean he didn't want to speak any more to you."

Yuna bit her lip, her mind spiraling into the endless possibilities. Elara's words, though logical, seemed too mundane to cover the complexities she had felt in that shared moment with Callum.

The next day, however, Yuna's focus was shifted when she encountered Maris during their shared herbology lesson. Maris, with her usual sharp gaze and calculated movements, worked methodically, her fingers nimble as she tended to the delicate herbs. Yuna, meanwhile, was more intuitive - tending quickly, and sometimes carelessly.

"You're going to crush the root," Maris said, her voice cool, as she watched Yuna wrestle with a particularly stubborn patch of valerian root. "You need to be gentle with them, not like some clumsy bear."

Yuna straightened up, her face flushing slightly. "I'm not clumsy," she retorted, a hint of challenge in her voice. "I just work quickly. It's more efficient."

Maris snorted, her face drawn into a displeased expression. "Efficient? You're just rushing. That's how mistakes happen. True skill requires precision, not speed." Her voice was laced with that same undercurrent of criticism that Yuna had come to know so well.

"Maybe I don't want to be precise," Yuna said, her hands tightening on her gardening trowel. "Maybe I like my magic wild. Untamed."

"Untamed? You call that chaotic, not untamed," Maris countered. "You're like a storm, unpredictable and destructive." Yuna bristled at the insult. "And you're just too uptight! Like the ground you are made of, you are rigid and unchanging."

Maris' eyes narrowed. "It is better to be rigid than to be all over the place."

"No it's not!" Yuna retorted.

Professor Meadowsweet, a gentle woman with a knack for calm, stepped between them, her face etched with concern. "Girls, is there a problem?"

Maris and Yuna glanced at each other for a moment, the air between them charged with unspoken tension. "No, Professor,"

Maris said, her voice smooth, her face a mask of politeness. "We were just having a... disagreement over gardening techniques."

Professor Meadowsweet raised an eyebrow, clearly not convinced. "Well, try to keep your 'disagreements' civil. These plants need to thrive, not suffer from your... energy." She then turned to direct the class. Yuna and Maris returned to their respective patches of the herb garden, their actions stiff and strained. Yuna felt a surge of anger, frustration boiling within her. Maris seemed determined to pick fault with everything she did, to undermine her every attempt at success. It was as if Maris felt threatened by her, as if her natural energy somehow challenged her view of the world.

As the days passed, the tension between Yuna and Maris continued to mount. In the sparring ring during defense class, their encounters were particularly explosive. Maris, with her precise earth magic, erected walls of stone and earth, forcing Yuna to use her speed and agility to evade her attacks. Yuna, in turn, unleashed bolts of pure energy, pushing Maris's defenses to their limits. Their clashes were a spectacle of raw power and intense, unwavering rivalry. During one particular sparring session, Maris pressed Yuna hard, forcing her back against the wall of the ring. Yuna, feeling cornered, unleashed a surge of untamed power, a burst of raw energy that caused Maris' earth wall to crumble, sending fragments of stone flying. The force of the blast threw Maris backwards, and she landed hard on the ground, her face contorted with a mixture of anger and shock.

"You could have hurt someone!" shouted one of the students.

Maris pushed herself back up, her gaze fixed on Yuna. "That was reckless, Yuna. You could have cost me serious injury. Your lack of control is dangerous."

Yuna, breathing heavily, felt a pang of remorse, but her anger was still simmering below the surface. "You were pushing me, Maris. You always do. I have to defend myself."

"Defend yourself?" Maris scoffed. " Or are you just showing off? You always have to be the center of attention."

"I don't want to be the center of attention!" Yuna retorted, her voice rising. "You're the one who is always challenging me, Maris. You try to make me look bad every chance you get."

"It's easy when you make it so obvious," Maris fired back. "You are all show and no substance."

"Oh, is being angry substance?" Yuna shot back.

The other students watched with bated breath as the confrontation escalated. Professor Thorne, their defense instructor, stepped into the ring, his face stern. "That's enough, both of you. This is a training ground, not a battleground. I'll expect you both to cool down before the next session. I don't want to see more of this nonsense." His voice was cold and firm, and the two girls fell silent immediately, not daring to challenge his authority.

As Yuna walked away from the sparring ring, her mind was a storm of conflicting emotions. She couldn't understand why Maris seemed to dislike her so intensely. Was it jealousy? Or was there something else she was missing? The friendship she had been hoping for with her fellow students were fracturing before her eyes, and she didn't know how to fix it. That evening, Yuna found herself wandering through the library, hoping to find some clarity amidst the endless rows of books and scrolls. Elara had gone to bed early, complaining of a headache, so Yuna was alone with her swirling thoughts. She pulled a book from the shelf, its spine marked with ancient symbols. She opened it idly, barely registering the words, her mind still consumed by her clashes with Maris, and the confusing interactions with Callum.

She jumped slightly when a voice startled her from her thoughts.

"Trouble with your incantations?" Callum asked, his voice soft, as he approached her desk.

Yuna looked up, surprised that he was there. "No," she said, lowering her gaze and closing the book. "Just thinking."

Callum sat down on the opposite side of the desk, his blue eyes searching her face. "Thinking about what?"

Yuna hesitated, unsure whether she should confide in him. But there was something about his calm demeanor, his quiet focus, that made her want to share her feelings. "It's just... I don't understand some people," she said, her voice low. "Like Maris. She seems to hate me for no reason."

Callum nodded, his gaze unwavering. "Maris has a particular way of viewing things. She sees challenges everywhere. It's not always about you." Yuna raised an eyebrow. "But it feels like it. She criticizes everything that I do, she pushes me in class, and she's always trying to make me feel bad."

Callum was silent for a moment, his gaze fixed on a distant spot. "Some people see the world as a competition," he said finally, his voice barely above a whisper. "They feel they need to be on top. They see others as a threat."

Yuna frowned. "But why? Why would she think that I'm a threat? I just want to be friends, but she treats everyone like enemies." "Not everyone, Yuna," Callum said, his eyes meeting hers. "She has friends that she cares about, just...she has her ways about her."

Yuna pondered his words, a new understanding dawning in her. Maris wasn't just a bully; she was driven by something deeper, something rooted in her own insecurities and fears. "I guess I just didn't realize. I thought she was just mean."

Callum nodded slowly. "Mean-ness isn't an end-point, it's an emotion or a reaction. There is always a reason."

Their conversation seemed to deepen after that. They spoke about their lessons, about the history of Aethelgard, and even about their hopes and dreams for the future. As they spoke, Yuna felt an unusual sense of connection, a comfortable silence that settled between them. It was as if Callum understood the turmoil within her, the questions that she couldn't quite articulate.

"You know, I don't normally talk to people like this," Yuna confessed, her cheeks flushing slightly. "You're very easy to talk to."

Callum gave her a small, almost shy smile. "I feel the same," he said, his voice soft. "You are... you are different, Yuna. You don't see the world like most people do. It's... refreshing."

Yuna laughed, a genuine, heartfelt sound. "I think you're different too, Callum. In a good way."

For a long time they talked, the air around them shimmering with a new understanding, a silent confirmation that something special was developing between them. By the time Yuna returned to her dorm, Elara was asleep in bed. Still, Yuna couldn't stop the smile from coming to her lips as she got ready for bed. The next morning, however, brought a sharp reminder that their budding connection did not exist in isolation. As Yuna entered the Grand Hall for breakfast, she noticed that Maris was watching her, her gaze cool and calculating. Yuna had expected Maris to have a look of anger or disdain, but the look on her face was different. Cold and calculating.

When Callum walked in, he turned to walk over to the table that Yuna and Elara were at, but Maris grabbed his arm.

"Callum, there's a seat here," she said, her voice overly sweet. "Come sit with us."

Callum looked at Yuna for a moment, a strange look on his face, before he moved over and joined the table of Maris and her friends. As he did, he didn't make eye contact with Yuna.

Yuna felt a pang of disappointment, a sharp reminder that her moment with Callum in the library was not the starting point of something magical. It was just a moment, and everything was back to how it was before. Throughout the day, Yuna tried to shake off the feeling of unease that had settled over her. She focused on her lessons, trying to ignore the glances that Maris threw her way, always accompanied by a subtle smirk. But during a particularly challenging session of practical magic, it became clear that something had indeed changed.

The task at hand was to create a temporary protective barrier using their combined elemental powers. Yuna, with her affinity for air and light, was paired with Elara, whose mastery was over earth and shadow. Maris, as always, was paired with Bren, their elemental forces forming a powerful duo of earth and fire.

CHAPTER V

The History of Shadows

The air in the corridor had shifted, growing colder with each step Yuna took. The flickering wall sconces, seemingly immune to the gentle currents that normally danced through the Academy's halls, seemed to cower, their light shrinking from an unseen presence. She'd been following the strange drafts, the whispered chills, for what felt like hours, since escaping the stuffy confines of her Advanced Arcanum studies. It had started, predictably, with a misplaced scroll in the library, a passage that seemed to pulse with dark energy even when safely tucked between the pages of a history codex. It spoke, not of the bright, established magic of the Academy, but of something... else. Something old, something hidden. And her curiosity, that constant, nagging itch within her, had to be scratched.

The corridor, unlike any she had seen before, was constructed from a dark, almost obsidian stone. Its surface was surprisingly smooth, cool to the touch, and absorbed the light rather than reflecting it. There were no tapestries, no inscriptions, no comforting signs of the Academy's daily bustle. Just stark, unadorned stone and the oppressive silence. Yuna's steps became hesitant, each echo sounding unnervingly loud in the stillness. Her gloved fingers traced the wall, seeking some clue, some break in the endless darkness. She found it in the form of a barely visible seam, a hairline fracture in the wall that seemed to tremble with a faint vibration. Pressing her hand flat against it, she could feel that same dark energy thrumming beneath her skin. It was like touching a frozen heartbeat. A series of soft clicks, like tumblers shifting in a lock, resonated deep within the wall, and a section of the obsidian façade swung inward, revealing a narrow passageway.

Yuna swallowed, her heart a frantic drum against her ribs. This was more than just the odd forgotten storage closet she half expected. This was a hidden chamber, deliberately concealed. Curiosity warred with caution, but curiosity, as always, won. She drew a deep breath, and with a final hesitant glance back at the empty corridor, stepped into the darkness. The passage sloped gently downwards, the air growing colder and heavier. The only illumination came from a pale, ethereal glow that seemed to emanate from the walls themselves. It wasn't a light she recognized; it was more like a faint luminescence as if the stones themselves were exhaling a cold, spectral breath. She kept one hand on the wall, the smooth obsidian surface a guide through the oppressive darkness. The silence intensified, broken only by the soft rhythmic beat of her pulse and the occasional scrape of her boots on the uneven floor.

The passageway opened into a circular chamber. The walls were still obsidian, but they were now punctuated with alcoves, each containing a single artifact. The ethereal glow was stronger here, casting long, dancing shadows across the chamber floor, giving a disorienting, almost dreamlike quality to the space. It wasn't just the objects that were old; it was the very air itself, thick with the weight of ages. Yuna felt like she had stumbled into a forgotten tomb, a secret repository of the Academy's darkest past.

She moved slowly into the chamber, her eyes scanning the alcoves, taking in each object in turn. There was a skeletal hand, its bones intricately carved with symbols she didn't recognise; a tarnished silver mirror that seemed to swallow the light rather than reflect it; and countless scrolls, bound in leather that looked brittle and cracked with age. She could sense the ancient magic radiating from these items, not the orderly magic she studied in her lessons, but something... raw. Something... untamed.

Yuna paused before a specific alcove, her breath catching in her throat. Inside sat a heavy, leather-bound tome, its cover embossed with a motif of a single, stylized eye. This wasn't the faded, crumbling leather of the other scrolls. This was dark, almost black, and felt unnervingly warm to the touch. It was as if the book itself was alive, pulsing with a barely contained energy. She knew, instinctively, that she had found something important. Something dangerous.

Fear whispered at the edges of her mind, but curiosity, along with a sense of inevitability, pushed it back. She couldn't ignore it. She reached for the tome, her fingers trembling slightly as she brushed against the dark leather. It felt almost as if the book was reaching out to her, inviting her, seducing her into its embrace.

She lifted the heavy tome from the alcove. It seemed to weigh more than its size would suggest, but Yuna found she had no trouble carrying it. She moved towards the centre of the chamber, the light from the walls coalescing around her, making the room feel less oppressive, if not less eerie. As she lowered herself to the cool stone floor, the weight of the book felt almost comforting in a strange way. This was clearly meant for her to find.

Carefully, her fingers, clad in the thin leather of her gloves, traced the edge of the cover, her gaze fixed on the single, all-seeing eye. This, she knew, was not just a book. It was a key. A key to secrets she had only begun to suspect.

With a deep breath, Yuna opened the tome.

The pages were not made of paper but of a strange, almost translucent material, like polished bone. The ink wasn't the usual black or brown, but a shimmering, almost liquid silver. The script was unlike anything she had ever encountered, intricate and flowing like a river, with symbols that seemed both ancient and disturbingly alive. Yet, as she stared at it, a strange thing happened. It was as if a part of her mind awoke, resonating with symbols. The script, which seconds ago had looked like an alien language, began to make sense. More than that understand, she felt it. This was no ordinary language she had stumbled upon, this was something... older.

The first pages spoke of the founding of the Academy, of the early mages who had built it on a foundation of knowledge and light. They had sought to understand the mysteries of the world, to harness its power for good. But those early days, she realized as she read on, were not without their shadows.

The narrative then shifted, the tone of the text growing darker. It spoke of a time before the establishment of the Academy, a time when magic was wild, untamed, and easily corrupted. Yuna traced the silver script with her finger, her eyes absorbing every detail. The book described a powerful being, a mage of unparalleled skill and intellect. His name, she soon discovered, was Aakari.

The name itself seemed to reverberate through the chamber, a whispered echo in the otherwise oppressive silence. Yuna found her breath catching in her throat, a cold shiver running down her spine. It was a name that resonated with a sense of foreboding, a name that felt both ancient and unnervingly present.

Aakari, according to the tome, was a master of magic, his understanding of the arcane arts was said to be far beyond even the most learned master. He delved into the deepest, most forbidden aspects of magic, pursuing knowledge beyond the boundaries of what was considered safe or ethical. He sought the source, the very root of magic itself. He was not content with simply manipulating the world; he wanted to unravel its very essence. Yuna read on, her fingers tracing the silver script as if it were a lifeline. The tome described Aakari's experiments, his increasingly dangerous explorations into the nature of reality. He had built towers of unholy power, manipulated the very fabric of existence, and pushed the boundaries of magic to their breaking point. His goal, she realized, was nothing less than the complete and utter mastery of the arcane. He sought not just understanding, but control.

He pushed the boundaries of magic, seeking control over everything he encountered. He delved into the nature of the Void, and beyond, not just seeking power but unraveling it. He was no longer interested in making the world better, in controlling the world through magic, but in simply controlling it... completely. It became, the book implied, an obsession. The text then spoke of the council of mages, those who had built the Academy and pursued knowledge through reason and understanding. They had become wary of Aakari's power, of the darkness that seemed to cling to him like a shroud. They saw his experiments as a threat, not just to themselves, but to the world itself. They pleaded with him to stop, to abandon his dangerous pursuits but he refused, calling them weak, naive fools. He couldn't understand their timidity, their willingness to remain ignorant.

The conflict between Aakari and the council escalated, becoming a battle not just of magic, but of ideologies. The council, representing order and reason, fought against Aakari's relentless pursuit of power and his increasingly twisted understanding of the arcane arts. There were no good guys, not really. The council was afraid, and Aakari was arrogant and blind. Both sides felt fully justified. The battle was devastating, the tome described a world on the brink of destruction. Aakari was not content with simply defeating the council. He sought to unmake the world itself, to reshape it in his twisted image. His magic, the book described with an undercurrent of horror, was not the vibrant, life-giving magic Yuna knew, it was something else. Something colder, emptier, and far more terrible.

Yuna felt a chill ran through her, not from the cold stone beneath her but the dark, terrible truth laid out before her in the ancient script. The mages of the council had faced an enemy who could manipulate the very fabric of reality, an enemy whose magic was not merely powerful, but corrupt. If not for what she read next, she would have considered that defeat was all but inevitable. The council, facing the possibility of utter destruction, made a decision. They wouldn't destroy Aakari, they wouldn't engage him in further, ultimately futile, direct combat. Instead, they used their understanding, their own carefully studied magic, to weave a powerful prison. Aakari, caught unaware, was banished from this reality, his consciousness confined to a realm beyond the veil of existence.

The text described the ritual, the incantations, and the immense magical effort that had gone into the creation of his prison. It was not a physical prison, but a spiritual one, a binding of his very essence. He was exiled, not into some far corner of the world, but out of the world and into the Void itself. He had become a shadow, a whisper, a dark echo in the void.

Yuna's fingers trembled as she finished reading the passage. The tome then went on to describe how, after Aakari's exile, the council had built the Academy, as a monument to the understanding and cautious use of magic. They sought to teach their students to respect the power they wielded, to learn from the mistakes of the past, and to never repeat the folly of Aakari. They had set up safeguards, wards, and protections that ensured that such dark knowledge was never to be discovered again, and that the mistakes of the past were never to be repeated.

The final pages of the tome were not filled with history but with a warning. A chilling declaration that Aakari was not dead. He could still hear the whispers of the world, and feel its currents of magic. His essence, though imprisoned, was not entirely extinguished. And the tome ended with a chilling phrase, a whisper of dread that seemed to echo through the chamber itself: "He will return." Yuna closed the tome, her hands shaking. The weight of its contents pressed down on her, a heavy burden of forbidden knowledge. Aakari was not just a myth, a legend of the past. He was a real, living, and potentially returning threat. He had been exiled, but a part of him remained, a shadow waiting to be unleashed.

She looked around the chamber, at the strange artifacts in the alcoves, and the cold, ethereal light that permeated the room. Her heart raced, a frantic drumbeat against her ribs. This was not just a hidden chamber; it was a prison of knowledge. A warning left behind by those who had come before, desperate to prevent the past from repeating itself. Yuna leaned back against the cold, smooth wall, her mind racing. The information in the book was shocking, terrifying even. But it also explained a lot. The strange currents she had felt, the whispers in the corridors, the unease that had been growing in the Academy. It was all linked to Aakari. He was not merely a distant threat, a figure of the past. He was, she realized, waking up.

And with that terrible conclusion, a new, far more terrifying idea took hold. She had only found this place a few hours ago, but what if she wasn't the first one to stumble across it? What if someone else, someone... more attuned to the darkness of Aakari, had already found it, already begun to understand? What if this was the reason he was returning, the foothold he needed to break free?

These thoughts sent a chill down her spine, colder than the stone at her back. It was one thing to read about a terrifyingly powerful dark mage from history - it was quite another to suddenly consider that he was, in some way, still there. She had thought that her quest for answers, her desire to learn all she could, was some kind of innocent curiosity. She now knew it was no longer just curiosity, it was a necessity. If she wanted to survive, the Academy to survive, she would need to understand Aakari. She needed to know everything.

She opened the tome once more, her fingers racing over the silver script. She needed to know more. What were his weaknesses? What did his magic look like? What could be done to prevent his return? She needed to become an expert. She needed to know all she could, and she needed to know it now.

She found the descriptions of Aakari's magic, it was not the type of elemental manipulation she had come to expect. It was described as a manipulation of the 'fundamental nature of things', a twisting of the very fabric of existence. His brand of magic was not about creation or even destruction, it was about 'un-making'. It was the undoing of purpose, the slow and insidious unraveling of everything. His magic was a corrosive force that sought to dissolve the world into the nothing he inhabited in the void.

The tome also mentioned his obsession with control, his arrogance, and his belief that he was the only one who truly understood the nature of magic. These weren't just personality flaws, she realized, they were potential weaknesses. A mind driven by arrogance could be made careless, and a mind focused solely on power could be blind to the smaller traps and tricks. And that, she realized, was where hope could be found. The hours flew by, each page she turned revealing another piece of the puzzle. She learned of the sacrifices the council had made, the desperate measures they had taken, to keep Aakari imprisoned. She learned about the wards that protected the Academy, and the subtle energies that ran beneath its foundations. She also began to recognize how these wards worked, how to bolster them, and most importantly, how to recognize when they might be failing.

The ethereal glow of the chamber began to dim, a sign that the dawn was approaching. Yuna realized, with a start, that she had been in the chamber all night, lost in the ancient world of the book. She had to get back, she had to return to her room, had to pretend like nothing had changed. But she knew, deep down, that nothing would ever be the same again. She had seen behind the veil, and she couldn't simply go back to her old life. She closed the tome once more, its dark leather cover feeling warm against her fingertips. She had learned more in one night than in all her years at the Academy. She now knew, but that knowledge was a responsibility. She couldn't tell anyone about this yet, not before she had a plan. She had to protect the Academy, and the world, from the shadow that was stirring in the dark.

As she stood to leave, she glanced back at the chamber, at the artifacts, and the pale light that seemed to dance on the walls. She could feel Aakari, not as a physical presence, but as an energy, a whisper, a dark promise that was carried on the wind. He was coming, she knew it, and she had to be ready. She slipped back into the hidden passage, the obsidian wall sliding shut behind her with a soft click. She was back in the regular corridors, the familiar smells of parchment and polished wood filling her senses. But she was not the same person who had entered it. She carried a secret, a terrible secret, and it burned within her like a fire.

Yuna made her way back to her room, her movements stiff, and her eyes tired. She had missed her classes, she knew, and she would face a stern lecture from her instructors. But those lectures, and all the other petty concerns of her old life, seemed insignificant compared to the threat that now lurked in the shadows.

As she slipped into her room, the first rays of dawn filtering through the window, she opened her study journal. She opened to a fresh page and in her neat, practiced script she wrote the words:

"The history of shadows has begun."

CHAPTER VI

Awakening Magic

The parchment crinkled softly in Yuna's hands, the ink still slightly damp. It wasn't just a list of spells – it was a key. A key to a world that had been hidden from her, a world now blossoming within her very being. The understanding, gleaned from ancient texts and late-night talks with Elara, had settled within her like a warm ember, ready to ignite. She finally grasped the fundamentals, the underlying principles that allowed magic to flow. It wasn't just reciting words; it was about intention, visualization, and the channeling of internal energy.

She looked out from the window of the library, the sprawling expanse of the Academy's grounds bathed in the golden light of early morning. Students were making their way to breakfast, their laughter, and chatter a muted symphony. Yuna felt a sense of detachment as if she were observing the world from behind a veil. The mundane seemed a little... dull, compared to the vibrant, pulsating energy that now hummed beneath her skin. A tentative smile touched her lips. It was time to practice.

She slipped the parchment into her satchel and made her way to the training grounds. Even at this early hour, the space was not entirely deserted. A few of the more dedicated students were already practicing, their spells crackling in the air. Yuna found an empty corner near the edge of the training circle. She closed her eyes, drawing a deep breath. She could feel it, the energy – a vibrant, tingling sensation that ran through her like an invisible current. She visualized the first spell she intended to practice: Lumen. A simple spell, but a fundamental one: a ball of light.

She focused, picturing the pure, white light, the essence of illumination, and whispered the incantation. "Lumes."

A small spark popped into existence between her palms. It flickered, hesitant, and then died out. Yuna frowned, her brow furrowing. She tried again. "Lumes." Another spark. Then, nothing.

She repeated the process several times, growing increasingly frustrated. The energy was there, she could feel it, but she couldn't seem to contain it, to shape it into the desired form. Frustrated, she exhaled and opened her eyes to see two figures standing in front of her, arms crossed, their expressions a mixture of amusement and concern. It was Callum and Kael.

"Having trouble, Yuna?" Callum inquired, his usual teasing tone present, but laced with a hint of genuine interest.

Kael chuckled. "You look like you're trying to make a fire with two wet sticks."

Yuna couldn't help but smile, despite her frustration. "Something like that," she admitted. "It's not as easy as Elara makes it seem."

"Magic rarely is," Callum agreed, stepping closer. "Let's see what you're doing wrong." He knelt beside her, his gaze focused and intense. "Tell me what you're feeling."

Yuna repeated the process, describing her sensations and her visualization. Callum listened intently, occasionally nodding or asking for clarification. When she finished, he looked thoughtful. "You're focusing too much on the words alone, and not enough on the image," he said. "Magic isn't just about repeating the right incantation. It's about feeling it, about believing it within your core. Imagine the light, visualize its form and its power, let that feeling flow through you, and then gently shape it with the incantation."

Yuna digested his words, feeling a flicker of understanding. "So it's more like... guiding the energy?"

Callum nodded. "Exactly."

Kael, who had been observing quietly, offered a different perspective. "And don't be so tense. Magic responds to calmness and clarity, not to frustration. It's like trying to catch a butterfly. If you chase it too hard, it will fly away."

Yuna took a deep, calming breath and tried again. She focused on the image of the small, bright sphere, picturing the way it would glow, the way it would illuminate the space around it. She imagined the energy flowing through her like a gentle stream, and whispered the incantation, "Lumes."

This time, the spark that appeared was different. It was stronger, more stable, and it began to grow, slowly at first, then steadily, forming a ball of pale light that hovered between her hands. It emitted a warm, soft glow, casting gentle shadows on the ground around them.

Yuna gasped, her eyes wide with surprise and delight. "I did it!"

Callum beamed at her, a flash of genuine pride in his expression. "You did it. See? We're naturals." He playfully bumped her shoulder, the usual light in his eyes reflecting a warmth that made her heart skip a beat. Kael clapped his hands, his own eyes sparkling. "Fantastic, Yuna! See, with a little guidance and a lot of patience, you'll be casting powerful spells in no time."

Yuna savored the moment, the warm light of the Lumen illuminating her face. This was just the beginning. She felt an incredible sense of excitement mixed with a touch of trepidation. This newfound power, this magic that now surged within her, was something she needed to understand, to control.

The following weeks turned into a whirlwind of training and study. Yuna, fuelled by her initial success, dedicated every spare moment to honing her abilities. She devoured books on spellcasting, experimented with various incantations, and practiced relentlessly with Callum and Kael. They became an inseparable trio, their bond strengthening with every shared training session. Callum, despite his natural talent, was surprisingly helpful and patient. He often offered words of encouragement when Yuna was struggling, sharing his methods and techniques. Kael, with her more analytical mind, would often point out flaws in their methods, suggesting alternative approaches. Their different perspectives both frustrated her sometimes but pushed her in different directions. Yuna discovered that she had a particular affinity for spells related to healing and light, while Callum excelled in combat-oriented magic. Kael, grounded and pragmatic, was adept at protective spells and enchanting. They were an unlikely combination, but each complemented the other, creating a synergistic whole. They began to train together as one, building up their team dynamic.

Yuna's understanding grew, not just with the practical applications of magic, but with its more esoteric aspects. She learned about the different schools of magic, the history behind the incantations, and the delicate balance that existed between the various forces. She also learned about the dangers of magic, the potential for corruption and misuse, the shadows that lingered on the edges of reality.

One evening, after a particularly grueling training session, Yuna sat alone in the library, surrounded by ancient tomes. She was studying a particularly dense text on the nature of magical energy when a peculiar passage caught her eye. It spoke of a 'stirring' – a feeling of unrest, of a dormant force awakening.

A chill ran down her spine as she read the words, a sense of unease settling in her stomach. The passage described how this stirring often manifested in dreams, in a blurring of the lines between reality and illusion. It was accompanied by a sense of dread, a feeling that something terrible was about to happen.

Yuna closed the book, a knot forming in her chest. She had been experiencing disturbing dreams lately, vivid and unsettling visions that left her feeling shaken and disoriented. In one dream, she saw a vast, empty plain covered in swirling shadows. In another, she witnessed a figure cloaked in darkness, its eyes burning with an unnatural light. She dismissed them as figments of her imagination, the result of her intense training and late nights, but now, reading this passage, she couldn't shake the feeling that there was more to them. That there was a reason behind them.

The following night, the dreams grew more vivid. She found herself standing in a dark forest, the air heavy with an oppressive silence. The trees were gnarled and twisted, their branches reaching out like skeletal fingers. She could feel a presence nearby, a malevolent force that seemed to watch her from the shadows. As she tried to move, she felt an invisible restraint holding her in place, as if the forest itself was trapping her. A figure emerged from the darkness. Tall and imposing, cloaked in black robes, its face obscured by shadows. But Yuna could sense the power radiating from it, a dark, terrifying energy that sent shivers down her spine. The figure reached out a hand, and Yuna felt a strange pull as if it was trying to draw her into the darkness. She cried out, her voice lost in the suffocating silence.

She woke up in a cold sweat, her heart pounding in her chest. The image of the cloaked figure was burned into her mind, its dark eyes staring into her soul. She sat up in bed, her hands trembling, and tried to rationalize the dream. It was just a dream, she told herself, just a product of her imagination, but the fear persisted, a cold, nagging dread that refused to let go. She knew she couldn't ignore it. The book, her dreams, the strange feeling in the pit of her stomach, it all pointed to something deeper, something more significant. She felt as though she was standing on the precipice of something, something huge that she wasn't ready for. The dreams continued, each one more intense than the last, and Yuna found herself growing increasingly withdrawn. She struggled to focus on her training, her mind constantly replaying the terrifying visions. She found herself observing the world around her differently as if she were seeing it through a layer of distortion.

Callum and Kael noticed the change in her behavior. They observed the shadows beneath her eyes, the tremor in her hands, and the subtle shifts in her mood. They grew concerned, increasingly worried about her, and tried to reach out, to offer their support.

"Yuna, you've been acting strange lately," Callum said one day when they were practicing on the training grounds. His blue eyes were intense with concern as he watched her fire off a spell. She had messed it up three times in a row.

Yuna avoided his gaze, trying to brush off his concern. "I'm fine, Callum. Just a little tired."

Kael stepped forward, her green eyes sharp. "Tired? You've been practically sleepwalking through training for the past week. Are you sure nothing is wrong?"

Yuna sighed, feeling a pang of guilt. She didn't want to burden them with her fears, didn't want to admit that she was being haunted by nightmares she couldn't explain. But she also knew that she couldn't continue to push them away.

"I've been having... dreams," she admitted, her voice barely a whisper. "Disturbing dreams. There's a figure, in the dark. It feels..." She struggled to find the right word. "It feels evil."

Callum and Kael exchanged a worried look. Kael took a step closer, her hand resting gently on Yuna's arm. "Do you want to talk about them?" Yuna hesitated but decided to share the details, recounting her visions, the dark forest, the silent world, and the cloaked figure that filled her with dread. As she spoke, she could see the concern growing in their eyes, turning to a deeper kind of fear.

Callum crossed his arms, his jaw clenched tightly. "That doesn't sound good, Yuna."

Kael nodded, her expression serious. "The Academy has strict protocols for dealing with dark magic. We need to report this."

Yuna shook her head, a sense of panic engulfing her. "No! We can't. What if they think I'm turning? What if they blame me?" The thought was terrifying. Her magic was new and fragile, she had worked too hard to be dismissed as a danger, a threat before she had even proven herself. "They won't, Yuna." Callum argued, "But we need to tell someone. Elara, maybe? She'd know what to do, wouldn't she?"

"But... what if she gets worried? What if she can't help?" Yuna's voice was filled with doubt.

Kael squeezed her arm gently. "We'll figure it out together, Yuna. We always do."

Yuna looked at them, her eyes filling with gratitude. They were her friends, her rock. They would stand by her no matter what. She took a deep breath, trying to quell the fear that was clawing at her chest. "Okay," she said, her voice slightly more assertive. "But we need to at least find out more before we go straight to the Academy."

From that point on, the trio began a clandestine investigation, delving into forbidden texts, and searching for clues about the nature of Yuna's dreams. They spent countless nights in the library, poring over ancient scriptures and cryptic prophecies. The knowledge they uncovered was unsettling, painting a picture of a looming darkness, a force that was once thought to be banished, but now, seemed to be stirring once again.

They learned about a being known as the Aakari, a powerful entity that fed on despair and chaos. It was said to have existed in the time before the Academy was built, a dark force that was eventually banished by the combined efforts of the greatest mages of that age. But according to the texts, the Aakari could never truly be destroyed; it could only be contained. And now, it seemed, that containment was weakening.

The discovery sent a new wave of fear through Yuna. She realized that her dreams weren't just figments of her imagination; they were a warning, a premonition of a terrible storm that was about to break. Not only did they point to a dark force but, more chillingly, it seemed it was specifically calling to her, to target her. Callum tried to reassure her, reminding her of her strength and potential. They vowed to stand by her side, to face this darkness together. But Yuna couldn't shake the feeling that she was walking a dangerous path and that her very soul was now at risk.

Despite the looming shadow, their bond continued to deepen. They became inseparable, their lives intertwined in a tapestry woven with magic and friendship. They were no longer just students; they were a team, a force to be reckoned with. Yuna found herself leaning more on Callum, his unwavering confidence and playful nature a welcome distraction from the darkness that threatened to engulf her. She admired his bravery, and his willingness to face any challenge head-on. And she couldn't deny the growing feelings she harbored for him, the way her heart fluttered whenever he smiled at her, the way her cheeks flushed when he playfully teased her.

Callum, in his way, was changing as well. The usual carefree facade was now mixed with a deeper sense of responsibility and seriousness. He was fiercely protective of Yuna, always watching out for her, ready to defend her against any threat. He was beginning to understand the depth of his feelings for her, the way she had somehow become the center of his world.

Kael was the grounded one. Her pragmatic nature and sharp wit kept them both in check. He was always ready with a logical explanation, a practical solution, and a comforting word of reassurance. He was the glue that held them together, the steady hand in a sea of uncertainty. He cared about both of her friends deeply and had grown protective of them, too. Their training sessions became more intense, their magic growing stronger with each passing day. They developed a unique fighting style, a blend of light and shadow, of offense and defense. They moved as one, their minds connected, anticipating each other's moves.

In one particular training session, they were practicing a complex spell that involved combining their energies into a single force. The spell was difficult, requiring precise coordination and a deep connection between their minds.

They began the incantation, their voices merging, creating a harmonious chant. As they continued, they could feel the energy building within them, a potent force that surged through their veins. They visualized their energies merging, creating a swirling vortex that spun in the center of the training circle. Suddenly, Yuna felt a strange sensation, as if she were no longer just herself. She felt a connection to Callum, to Kael, as if their thoughts, their feelings, were flowing into her mind. She could sense their energy merging with hers, creating a powerful synergy.

The vortex in the center of the circle began to glow, first with a pale light, then with a brilliant radiance. The energy that emanated from it was intense, warm, and incredibly powerful. It washed over them, filling them with a sense of euphoria and belonging. When the spell concluded, the three of them stood breathless, their minds still buzzing with the residual energy. They looked at each other, their eyes wide with awe and wonder.

Callum was the one to break the silence. "Did you feel that?" he asked, his voice full of amazement.

Kael nodded her expression a mixture of surprise and understanding. "It was as if... we were all connected."

Yuna looked at them, a smile slowly spreading across her face. "I felt it too," she said. "It was incredible." She had never felt anything like that before. The experience, while intense, was also extremely comforting. She had never felt so safe, so secure. The experience reaffirmed the strength of their bond, demonstrating that their friendship was more powerful than even they had imagined. They were beginning to understand the potential of their combined power, and the incredible things they could achieve together. They were a unit, a team, a force to be reckoned with.

Despite the growing strength of their bond, the shadows continued to linger. The dreams grew more intense, the whispers of darkness louder. seemed to be drawing closer, its presence a cold, suffocating blanket that threatened to smother their lives. Yuna found herself growing more and more anxious, her sleep becoming increasingly sporadic. She would wake up in the middle of the night, her heart racing, the image of the cloaked figure branded into her mind. She tried to find solace in the company of Callum and Kael, but even their presence couldn't completely dispel the dread that consumed her.

She began to question herself, wondering if she was strong enough to face the darkness that was coming her way. She was a mage, yes, but she was also a girl. One who was still finding her place in the world. She was surrounded by shadows both externally and internally. Callum and Kael tried their best to support her, but they were worried. They were frustrated by their inability to put an end to her nightmares, to banish the shadows that seemed intent on consuming her. Their hope was slowly waning, replaced by a quiet kind of desperation.

One evening, they were in the library, searching for more clues in a particularly old and worn book. Yuna was slumped against the wall, her head in her hands. She had barely slept for days and was struggling to concentrate.

Callum sat beside her, putting his arm around her and pulling her in. "You need to rest," he said, gently.

Yuna shook her head, her eyes filled with grief. "I can't. Not while... it's still out there."

Kael was studying a page, her brow furrowed in concentration, "We're close, Yuna. I can feel it."

Yuna sighed, "What if we fail? What if we aren't strong enough?"

Callum squeezed her shoulder. "You are strong enough, Yuna. You're the strongest person I know."

His words were a balm to her soul, a wave of warmth that spread through her. She leaned into his touch, finding comfort in his presence. Kael gasped, her eyes wide with realization. "I think... I think I've found something." She pushed the book across to them, her finger pointing to a series of symbols and text.

The text appeared to be a ritual, a way to temporarily banish the Aakari, to push it back into the darkness from which it emerged. The symbols were ancient and complex, almost illegible.

"This might be it," Kael said hopefully, her voice trembling with emotion.

Callum leaned in closer, examining the text. "If we're going to try this, we need to be careful. It says that it's risky and that the slightest mistake could have dire consequences." Yuna had a sudden sense of decisiveness. She had had enough of the fear and anxiety. She had to face it. "Then we'll just have to make sure we don't make any mistakes."

CHAPTER VII

The Trials of Eldoria

The air was alive with excitement as the Harvest Moon Festival approached. The academy, normally a place of studious calm, was abuzz with anticipation. Students from all four houses –Lumina, Umbra, Chronus, and finally, Arcana – were busy preparing for the magical tournament that would be the centerpiece of the festival. The tournament, known as the Trials of Eldoria, was a time-honored tradition that pitted the best young mages against each other in a series of magical challenges.

As the students trained and honed their skills, tensions began to grow. Rivalries that had been simmering beneath the surface for months began to escalate, and the atmosphere in the academy grew increasingly charged. Whispers of a sinister plot to disrupt the festival began to circulate, and many wondered if the Trials of Eldoria would be more than just a friendly competition. Professor Lirien, the head of the magical arts department, stood at the front of the grand auditorium, surveying the crowd of students before him. "The Trials of Eldoria are a time for us to come together and celebrate our magical heritage," he said, his voice ringing out across the room. "But they are also a time for competition, and I expect to see every one of you giving your all to represent your house and your fellow students."

The students erupted into cheers and applause, their excitement and enthusiasm palpable. But amidst the jubilation, some were not so sure. Rumors had been circulating about a dark force that was seeking to disrupt the festival, and some students were beginning to wonder if the Trials of Eldoria were more than just a simple competition. Yuna, a young mage from the Aerius house, was one of those who was feeling uneasy. She had always loved the Harvest Moon Festival, and the Trials of Eldoria were her favorite part of the celebrations. But this year, something felt off. She couldn't quite put her finger on it, but she had a nagging sense of unease that she couldn't shake.

As she left the auditorium, Yuna was approached by Callum, a fellow member of her team(As they had to perform in triplets). "Hey, Yuna, what's wrong?" Callum asked, noticing the look of concern on her face. "You seem a bit distracted."

Yuna hesitated, unsure of how to express her feelings. "I don't know, Callum," she said finally. "I just have a bad feeling about this year's Trials. I've been hearing rumors about a dark force that's trying to disrupt the festival, and I'm starting to wonder if there's more to the Trials than just a simple competition."Callum's expression turned serious. "I've heard those rumors too," he said. "But I'm sure it's just gossip and speculation. The professors would never let anything happen to us." Yuna nodded, trying to reassure herself. But as she walked back to her dormitory, she couldn't shake the feeling that something was off. She decided to do some digging, to see if she could uncover any information about the rumors that were circulating.

As she delved deeper into the mystery, Yuna began to uncover some disturbing clues. She spoke to other students who had heard the rumors, and she discovered that several of them had experienced strange and unexplained occurrences in the days leading up to the festival. Some had reported finding strange symbols etched into the walls of the academy, while others had spoken of hearing eerie whispers in the dead of night.

Yuna led herself to the Ancient Room, where she stumbled upon another ancient tome bound in black leather. The book was adorned with strange symbols and markings that seemed to shimmer and glow in the dim light of the library. As she opened the book, Yuna felt a chill run down her spine. The pages were filled with dark and foreboding text, speaking of a powerful and malevolent force that threatened to destroy the balance of magic in the world.

Suddenly, the lights in the library flickered and dimmed, and Yuna felt a presence behind her. She turned to see a figure cloaked in shadows, its eyes glowing with an otherworldly energy. "You shouldn't be here," the figure hissed, its voice like a cold wind. "You shouldn't be meddling in things you don't understand." Yuna tried to run, but her feet seemed rooted to the spot. The figure began to move closer, its eyes burning with an intense and malevolent energy. Just as all hope seemed lost, the library was filled with a blinding light, and the figure vanished into thin air.

Yuna stumbled backward, gasping for breath. She realized that she had stumbled into something much bigger and more complex than she had ever imagined. The Trials of Eldoria were not just a simple competition – they were a battleground in a war between light and darkness, and Yuna had just become a key player in the struggle.

As the days passed, Yuna found herself drawn deeper into the mystery. She discovered that the dark force that was seeking to disrupt the festival was known as the Shadow Syndicate, a powerful and secretive organization that had been hiding in the shadows for years. The Syndicate was determined to destroy the balance of magic in the world, and the Trials of Eldoria were the key to their plan.

Yuna knew that she had to act fast. She gathered Kael and Callum. Together, they hatched a plan to stop the Shadow Syndicate and save the Harvest Moon Festival.

But as they delved deeper into the heart of the mystery, they realized that the Syndicate was more powerful and more ruthless than they had ever imagined. The students were in grave danger, and the fate of the academy hung in the balance. The night of the Trials of Eldoria arrived, and the academy was filled with excitement and anticipation. The students had spent weeks preparing for the tournament, and the air was electric with tension. But amidst the jubilation, Yuna and her friends knew that they were in for the fight of their lives.

The Trials began with a series of magical challenges, each one designed to test the student's skills and abilities. But as the competition heated up, it became clear that something was amiss. The Shadow Syndicate had infiltrated the tournament, and their agents were secretly manipulating the outcome.

The triplets fought bravely, using all of their magical skills to try and outmaneuver the Syndicate's agents. But despite their best efforts, they found themselves facing off against an enemy that seemed almost invincible.

As the final challenge approached, Yuna realized that the fate of the academy hung in the balance. The Shadow Syndicate was determined to destroy the balance of magic in the world, and the Trials of Eldoria were the key to their plan. Yuna and her friends were the only ones who could stop them, but the odds were stacked against them. The final challenge was a duel between the last two students standing – Yuna and a mysterious figure who was revealed to be a powerful agent of the Shadow Syndicate. The duel was fierce and intense, with both sides trading blows and neither gaining the upper hand.

But just as it seemed that the outcome was uncertain, Yuna remembered the words of an ancient prophecy that she had discovered in her research. The prophecy spoke of a powerful and ancient magic that would be unleashed when the balance of magic in the world was threatened. Yuna realized that she was the key to unlocking this magic, and with a surge of confidence and determination, she launched a final and decisive attack.

The agent of the Shadow Syndicate was defeated, and the balance of magic in the world was saved. The Harvest Moon Festival was a success, and the academy was filled with joy and celebration. Yuna and her friends had saved the day, and they were hailed as heroes. But as they stood on the stage, basking in the adoration of their fellow students, Yuna couldn't shake the feeling that the Shadow Syndicate was still out there, waiting and watching. The Trials of Eldoria may have been won, but the war between light and darkness was far from over. Yuna and her friends had emerged victorious, but they knew that they would have to remain vigilant, for the forces of darkness would not give up easily. With this, the first day of the Trials ended

69

CHAPTER VIII

Whispers of Aakari

The second day of the festival approached had been a long-awaited event in the land of Eldoria. For weeks, the townspeople had been preparing for the grand celebration, which marked the summer solstice and the longest day of the year. The streets were adorned with vibrant lanterns, and the smell of sweet pastries and roasted meats filled the air. Yuna, Kael, and Callum had been looking forward to the festival for what felt like an eternity, and they were determined to make the most of it(Due of facing more darkened spirits).

As the sun began to set on the day of the festival, the group of friends made their way to the town square. The atmosphere was electric, with people of all ages laughing and dancing together. Yuna, with her Wavy hair and bright smile, was in her element, twirling and spinning to the rhythm of the music. Callum, with his brooding good looks and quiet confidence, watched over the group with a keen eye, ever vigilant for any signs of trouble. Kael, with his quick wit and mischievous grin, was busy trying to convince the festival vendors to give him free samples of their wares.

As the night wore on, the storm that had been brewing on the horizon finally began to make its presence known. Dark clouds gathered, and a loud clap of thunder boomed through the sky. The music and laughter faltered, and the crowd began to murmur with concern. Yuna, Kael, and Callum exchanged nervous glances, sensing that something was amiss. At first, it was just a faint whisper, a soft rustling of leaves and a gentle creaking of trees. But as the storm intensified, the whispers grew louder, more urgent. It was as if the wind itself was trying to convey a message, to warn the people of Eldoria of some impending danger. Yuna, with her sensitive ears and quick mind, was the first to pick up on the whispers. She frowned, concentrating on the sound, trying to make out what was being said.

"Aakari," the wind whispered. "Aakari is coming."

Yuna's eyes snapped towards Kael and Callum, her face pale with concern. "Did you hear that?" she asked, her voice barely above a whisper.

Kael's eyes narrowed, his gaze scanning the crowd. "Hear what?" he asked, his voice low and even.

"The wind," Yuna replied, her eyes locked on Kael's. "It's whispering something. A name. Aakari."

Callum's eyes widened, his face lighting up with excitement. "Aakari?" he repeated. "Isn't that the name of the ancient sorcerer who was said to have wielded the power of the elements?"

Yuna nodded, her mind racing. "That's the one," she said. "But what does it mean? Why is the wind whispering his name?" As if in response, the storm surged forward, the winds howling and the lightning flashing across the sky. The crowd began to panic, screaming and running for cover. Yuna, Kael, and Callum were swept up in the chaos, struggling to stay on their feet as the storm raged on.

It was then that they saw it: a dark figure, standing at the edge of the town square. The figure was tall and imposing, its presence seeming to draw the very light out of the air. Yuna, Kael, and Callum exchanged a nervous glance, sensing that they were in the presence of something truly powerful.

As they watched, the figure began to move towards them, its pace slow and deliberate. The whispers in the wind grew louder, more urgent, and Yuna felt a shiver run down her spine. She knew, without a doubt, that they were in grave danger.

"Aakari," the wind whispered, the name echoing through the stormy night. "Aakari is coming."

The figure drew closer, its presence filling the air with an unspeakable evil. Yuna, Kael, and Callum stood frozen, unsure of what to do. And then, just as suddenly as it had begun, the storm stopped. The winds died down, the lightning ceased, and an eerie silence fell over the town square.

The figure stood before them, its eyes glowing with an otherworldly energy. Yuna, Kael, and Callum felt a surge of fear, knowing that they were face to face with a power that was beyond their wildest imagination.

"Who are you?" Yuna asked, her voice barely above a whisper.

The figure did not respond. Instead, it reached out a hand, its fingers closing around Yuna's wrist like a vice. Yuna felt a jolt of pain, and then she was flooded with visions and images, a torrent of information that threatened to overwhelm her.

She saw Aakari, the ancient sorcerer, wielding the power of the elements with ease. She saw the destruction he had wrought, the cities he had reduced to rubble, the lives he had destroyed. And she saw the prophecy, the warning that had been whispered in the wind.

Aakari was coming, the prophecy said. Aakari would bring destruction and chaos, and only those who were pure of heart and strong of spirit would be able to stand against him. As the visions faded, Yuna found herself back in the town square, the figure still grasping her wrist. She looked up at Kael and Callum, her eyes wide with fear.

"We have to get out of here," she said, her voice shaking. "We have to warn the others."

Callum nodded, his face set in a determined expression. "We'll get to the bottom of this," he said. "We'll find out what's going on, and we'll stop it."

Kael nodded, his eyes gleaming with excitement. "And we'll start by investigating the whispers," he said. "We'll find out what's behind the strange occurrences, and we'll put a stop to it."

Together, the three friends set off into the unknown, determined to unravel the mystery of Aakari and the whispers in the wind. They knew that it wouldn't be an easy task, but they were ready for whatever lay ahead. As they walked, the darkness seemed to press in around them, the shadows cast by the flickering torches twisting and writhing like living things. Yuna shivered, despite the warmth of the summer evening, and Kael put a reassuring arm around her shoulders.

"We'll get through this," he said, his voice low and steady. "We'll face whatever is coming, and we'll emerge victorious."

Yuna smiled, feeling a surge of gratitude towards her friends. She knew that she could always count on Callum, no matter what dangers lay ahead. And with Kael by their side, she felt a sense of hope, a sense that together, they could overcome anything. The journey ahead would be fraught with peril, but Yuna, Kael, and Callum were ready. They were ready to face whatever lay ahead, to unravel the mystery of Aakari and the whispers in the wind. And they were ready to emerge victorious, their bond and their determination guiding them through the darkest of times.

As they walked, the whispers in the wind grew fainter, the darkness seeming to recede before them. Yuna felt a sense of peace settles over her, a sense that they were on the right path. And she knew that no matter what lay ahead, she would face it with courage and strength, her friends by her side.

The storm may have passed, but the journey was far from over. Yuna, Kael, and Callum had only just begun to unravel the mystery of Aakari, and they knew that the road ahead would be long and treacherous. But they were ready, their hearts filled with hope and their spirits unbroken.

And so, with the whispers of Aakari still echoing in their minds, they pressed on, into the unknown, ready to face whatever lay ahead.

CHAPTER IX

The Gathering Storm

The magic that had infused with the air during the festival, a palpable and exhilarating energy that had seemed to pulse with the rhythm of the music, had waned.

As she walked through the quieting streets, Yuna felt an inexplicable pull, a call to venture into the unknown. She had always been drawn to the mysterious and the unexplored, and now she felt an overwhelming urge to explore the depths of the forest, to uncover secrets that had lain hidden for centuries.

Kael and Callum, her closest friends and companions, sensed her unease and fell into step beside her. "What's wrong, Yuna?" Kael asked, his eyes scanning the surrounding streets as if searching for some hidden threat.

"I don't know," Yuna admitted, her voice barely above a whisper. "I just feel...restless. Like there's something out there, waiting for me."

Callum's eyes narrowed, his gaze intensifying as he searched Yuna's face. "You're not thinking of going into the forest, are you?" he asked, his tone laced with a mixture of concern and curiosity.

Yuna hesitated, unsure of how to respond. She had been feeling the call of the forest for days, a siren's song that seemed to grow louder and more insistent with each passing hour. But she knew that the forest was a place of darkness and shadow, a realm of ancient magic and hidden dangers. "I don't know," she said finally, her voice barely above a whisper. "But I feel like I have to try. I feel like there's something out there, something that's been waiting for me all along."

Kael and Callum exchanged a glance, their faces set with determination. "We'll come with you," Kael said, his voice firm and resolute. "We'll face whatever is out there, together."

And with that, the three of them set off into the unknown, venturing into the depths of the forest with a sense of trepidation and wonder. The trees loomed above them, their branches creaking and swaying in the gentle breeze like skeletal fingers. The air was thick with the scent of damp earth and decaying leaves, a primordial smell that seemed to speak of ancient secrets and forgotten lore.

As they walked, the silence between them grew, until it seemed to become a living, breathing thing. Yuna felt the weight of the forest's gaze upon her, a sense of being watched and waited for. She shivered, despite the warmth of the summer evening, and quickened her pace, her heart pounding in her chest like a drum. The ruins lay hidden deep within the forest, a place of crumbling stone and overgrown vegetation. Yuna had heard stories of the ruins, whispers of a ancient civilization that had once flourished in this very spot. She had always been fascinated by the tales, and now, as she approached the ruins, she felt a sense of awe and wonder.

The entrance to the ruins was a massive stone doorway, covered in vines and moss. The doors themselves were long gone, lost to the ravages of time and weather. But the doorway remained, a testament to the ingenuity and craftsmanship of the long-lost civilization that had built this place. Yuna felt a shiver run down her spine as she stepped through the doorway, her eyes adjusting to the dim light within. The air was thick with dust and the scent of age, a musty smell that seemed to cling to every surface like a damp shroud. She coughed, her lungs protesting the dry air, and looked around, taking in the sights and sounds of the ruins.

The interior of the ruins was a maze of crumbling corridors and chambers, a labyrinthine complex that seemed to stretch on forever. Yuna wandered the halls, her footsteps echoing off the stone walls as she explored the ancient structures. She felt a sense of wonder and awe, a sense of discovery that was both exhilarating and terrifying.

As she walked, Yuna began to notice strange symbols etched into the walls, intricate patterns that seemed to pulse with a faint, otherworldly glow. She reached out a hand, her fingers tracing the curves and lines of the symbols, and felt a sudden jolt of energy, a surge of power that seemed to course through her veins like liquid fire.

Kael and Callum caught up to her, their faces set with concern. "Yuna, what's going on?" Kael asked, his voice low and urgent. "You look like you've seen a ghost."

Yuna shook her head, trying to clear the cobwebs. "I don't know," she admitted, her voice barely above a whisper. "I just feel...connected, somehow. Like I've been here before, even though I know I haven't."

Callum's eyes narrowed, his gaze intensifying as he searched Yuna's face. "You're not thinking of the visions, are you?" he asked, his tone laced with a mixture of curiosity and concern.

Yuna hesitated, unsure of how to respond. She had been experiencing strange visions, fragments of images and sounds that seemed to come from nowhere and everywhere at the same time. She had tried to ignore them, to push them to the back of her mind, but they had grown more insistent, more vivid, until she could hardly ignore them anymore.

"I don't know," she said finally, her voice barely above a whisper. "But I feel like there's something trying to tell me, something that's been trying to reach me for a long time."

Kael and Callum exchanged a glance, their faces set with determination. "We'll help you figure it out," Kael said, his voice firm and resolute. "We'll face whatever is out there, together."

And with that, the three of them continued on, deeper into the ruins, searching for answers to the questions that had been haunting Yuna for so long. The symbols on the walls seemed to grow more frequent, more intense, until Yuna felt like she was walking through a maze of glowing, pulsing energy.

The air grew colder, the shadows deepening and twisting until they seemed to take on a life of their own. Yuna felt a sense of unease, a sense of being watched and waited for. She shivered, despite the warmth of the summer evening, and quickened her pace, her heart pounding in her chest like a drum.

And then, suddenly, they were there, standing in a vast, cavernous space that seemed to stretch up to the stars. The ceiling was lost in darkness, a vaulted expanse of stone and shadow that seemed to swallow the light whole. The walls were lined with ancient artifacts, relics of a long-lost civilization that seemed to whisper secrets to the wind.

Yuna felt a sense of awe and wonder, a sense of discovery that was both exhilarating and terrifying. She wandered the space, her eyes drinking in the sights and sounds of the ancient relics. And then, suddenly, she saw it, a glowing crystal that seemed to pulse with an otherworldly energy.

The crystal was nestled in a bed of black stone, surrounded by a halo of faint, pulsing light. Yuna felt a sense of recognition, a sense of knowing that she had seen this crystal before, even though she knew she hadn't. She reached out a hand, her fingers tracing the curves and lines of the crystal, and felt a sudden jolt of energy, a surge of power that seemed to course through her veins like liquid fire.

Kael and Callum caught up to her, their faces set with concern. "Yuna, what's going on?" Kael asked, his voice low and urgent. "You look like you've seen a ghost."

Yuna shook her head, trying to clear the cobwebs. "I don't know," she admitted, her voice barely above a whisper. "I just feel...connected, somehow. Like I've been here before, even though I know I haven't."

Callum's eyes narrowed, his gaze intensifying as he searched Yuna's face. "You're thinking of the visions, are you?" he asked, his tone laced with a mixture of curiosity and concern. Yuna hesitated, unsure of how to respond. She had been experiencing strange visions, fragments of images and sounds that seemed to come from nowhere and everywhere at the same time. She had tried to ignore them, to push them to the back of her mind, but they had grown more insistent, more vivid, until she could hardly ignore them anymore.

"I don't know," she said finally, her voice barely above a whisper. "But I feel like there's something trying to tell me, something that's been trying to reach me for a long time."

Kael and Callum exchanged a glance, their faces set with determination. "We'll help you figure it out," Kael said, his voice firm and resolute. "We'll face whatever is out there, together."

And with that, the three of them stood there, frozen in time, as the crystal began to glow with an intense, pulsing light. The air seemed to vibrate with energy, a humming noise that seemed to grow louder and more intense with each passing moment.

Yuna felt herself being drawn into the crystal, a sense of being pulled apart and put back together again. She saw visions of the past, fragments of images and sounds that seemed to come from nowhere and everywhere at the same time. She saw a great and terrible war, a conflict that had ravaged the land and left deep scars. She saw a powerful and ancient magic, a force that had been wielded by a long-lost civilization.And she saw herself, standing at the center of it all, a key player in a drama that had been unfolding for centuries. Yuna felt a sense of wonder and awe, a sense of discovery that was both exhilarating and terrifying. She knew that she had stumbled into something much bigger than herself, something that would change her life forever.

As the visions faded, Yuna found herself back in the ruins, standing beside Kael and Callum. The crystal was still glowing, but the light was fainter now, a soft pulse that seemed to beat in time with her own heart.

"What did you see?" Kael asked, his voice low and urgent.

Yuna shook her head, trying to clear the cobwebs. "I don't know," she admitted, her voice barely above a whisper. "I saw visions of the past, fragments of images and sounds. I saw a great and terrible war, a conflict that had ravaged the land and left deep scars. I saw a powerful and ancient magic, a force that had been wielded by a long-lost civilization."

Callum's eyes narrowed, his gaze intensifying as he searched Yuna's face. "And what about you?" he asked, his tone laced with a mixture of curiosity and concern. "What did you see about yourself?"

Yuna hesitated, unsure of how to respond. She had seen herself standing at the center of it all, a key player in a drama that had been unfolding for centuries. She had seen a powerful and ancient magic, a force that had been wielded by a long-lost civilization.

"I saw myself," she said finally, her voice barely above a whisper. "I saw myself standing at the center of it all, a key player in a drama that has been unfolding for centuries. I saw a great and terrible war, a conflict that had ravaged the land and left deep scars. And I saw a powerful and ancient magic, a force that had been wielded by a long-lost civilization."

Kael and Callum exchanged a glance, their faces set with determination. "We'll help you figure it out," Kael said, his voice firm and resolute. "We'll face whatever is out there, together."

And with that, the three of them stood there, frozen in time, as the crystal continued to glow with a soft, pulsing light. The air seemed to vibrate with energy, a humming noise that seemed to grow louder and more intense with each passing moment.

Yuna felt herself being drawn into the crystal, a sense of being pulled apart and put back together again. She knew that she had stumbled into something much bigger than herself, something that would change her life forever. And she knew that she would never be the same again, that she would always be haunted by the visions of the past and the magic that had been wielded by a long-lost civilization.

As they stood there, the crystal began to glow with an intense, pulsing light. The air seemed to vibrate with energy, a humming noise that seemed to grow louder and more intense with each passing moment. Yuna felt herself being drawn into the crystal, a sense of being pulled apart and put back together again.

And then, suddenly, everything went black.

When Yuna came to, she was lying on the stone floor, her head throbbing with pain. Kael and Callum were standing over her, their faces set with concern.

"Yuna, what happened?" Kael asked, his voice low and urgent.

Yuna shook her head, trying to clear the cobwebs. "I don't know," she admitted, her voice barely above a whisper. "I saw visions of the past, fragments of images and sounds. I saw a great and terrible war, a conflict that had ravaged the land and left deep scars. I saw a powerful and ancient magic, a force that had been wielded by a long-lost civilization."

Callum's eyes narrowed, his gaze intensifying as he searched Yuna's face. "And what about you?" he asked, his tone laced with a mixture of curiosity and concern. "What did you see about yourself?"

Yuna hesitated, unsure of how to respond. She had seen herself standing at the center of it all, a key player in a drama that had been unfolding for centuries. She had seen a powerful and ancient magic, a force that had been wielded by a long-lost civilization.

"I saw myself," she said finally, her voice barely above a whisper. "I saw myself standing at the center of it all, a key player in a drama that has been unfolding for centuries. I saw a great and terrible war, a conflict that had ravaged the land and left deep scars. And I saw a powerful and ancient magic, a force that had been wielded by a long-lost civilization."

Kael and Callum exchanged a glance, their faces set with determination. "We'll help you figure it out," Kael said, his voice firm and resolute. "We'll face whatever is out there, together."

And with that, the three of them stood up, brushing themselves off. The crystal was still glowing, but the light was fainter now, a soft pulse that seemed to beat in time with Yuna's own heart.

As they walked out of the ruins, Yuna felt a sense of wonder and awe, a sense of discovery that was both exhilarating and terrifying. She knew that she had stumbled into something much bigger than herself, something that would change her life forever. And she knew that she would never be the same again, that she would always be haunted by the visions of the past and the magic that had been wielded by a long-lost civilization.

The forest was quiet and still, the trees looming above them like sentinels. Yuna felt a sense of peace, a sense of calm that seemed to wash over her like a wave. She knew that she had found something important, something that would help her unlock the secrets of the past.

As they walked, the trees seemed to grow taller and closer, their branches tangling together above their heads. Yuna felt a sense of wonder, a sense of discovery that was both exhilarating and terrifying. She knew that she had stumbled into something much bigger than herself, something that would change her life forever.

And then, suddenly, they heard it, a low rumbling noise that seemed to grow louder and more intense with each passing moment. Yuna felt a sense of fear, a sense of uncertainty that seemed to grip her heart.

"What's that?" she asked, her voice barely above a whisper.

Kael and Callum exchanged a glance, their faces set with concern. "I don't know," Kael said, his voice low and urgent. "But I think we should get out of here, now."

And with that, the three of them turned and ran, the rumbling noise growing louder and more intense with each passing moment. Yuna felt a sense of fear, a sense of uncertainty that seemed to grip her heart. She knew that she had stumbled into something much bigger than herself, something that would change her life forever. As they ran, the trees seemed to blur together, their branches tangling together above their heads. Yuna felt a sense of wonder, a sense of discovery that was both exhilarating and terrifying. She knew that she had found something important, something that would help her unlock the secrets of the past.

And then, suddenly, they were somewhere they didn't know. Yuna felt a sense of relief, a sense of safety that seemed to wash over her like a wave. She knew that she had found something important, something that would help her unlock the secrets of the past.

As they walked through the area, Yuna felt a sense of wonder, a sense of discovery that was both exhilarating and terrifying. She knew that she had stumbled into something much bigger than herself, something that would change her life forever. And she knew that she would never be the same again, that she would always be haunted by the visions of the past and the magic that had been wielded by a long-lost civilization.

she took out the old tomb finding more that they were almost in the heart of the forest finding that it is where the remants of Aakari's prison were there so they all decided to take rest for the night and then move on

Yuna felt a sense of fear, a sense of uncertainty that seemed to grip her heart. She knew that she had stumbled into something much bigger than herself, something that would change her life forever. And she knew that she would never be the same again, that she would always be haunted by the visions

CHAPTER X

The Heart of the Forest

Deep in Eldoria's heart, the trees grew taller and the underbrush thicker, as if the forest itself was trying to conceal the secrets that lay within. Yuna, Callum, and Kael had been traveling for days, navigating through the dense foliage with the aid of the ancient maps and cryptic clues that had led them to this point. The air was heavy with the scent of damp earth and decaying leaves, and the silence was oppressive, punctuated only by the occasional snapping of twigs and the soft rustling of small creatures through the underbrush.

As they walked, the trees seemed to grow closer together, forming a canopy overhead that filtered the sunlight and cast the forest floor in a dim, emerald green gloom. Yuna felt a shiver run down her spine, as if they were being watched by unseen eyes. She glanced at Kael, who walked beside her, his hand on the hilt of his sword. He caught her eye and nodded, his expression grim.

They had been searching for weeks, following every lead, every hint, every rumor that might bring them closer to their goal. And finally, after all this time, they had found it – the remnants of Aakari's ancient prison, hidden deep in the heart of the forest.

The prison itself was a massive structure, built from blocks of black stone that seemed to absorb the light around them. The walls were covered in intricate carvings, depicting scenes of great battles and powerful magic. Yuna felt a thrill of excitement as she reached out to touch the stone, feeling the weight of history and power that emanated from it.

According to legend, Aakari had been imprisoned here for centuries, bound by powerful magic and ancient spells. But the legends also hinted at a prophecy, one that was tied to Yuna's own lineage. It was said that she was the key to either binding

Aakari forever or unleashing him upon the realm once more.

As they explored the prison, Yuna couldn't shake the feeling that they were being led deeper into a trap. The air was thick with the scent of decay and corruption, and she could feel the weight of Aakari's presence bearing down upon her. She glanced at Kael, who was examining the carvings on the wall.

"What do you make of this?" he asked, his voice low and serious.

Yuna walked over to join him, studying the carvings. They depicted a great battle, with powerful sorcerers and warriors clashing in a frenzy of steel and magic. At the center of the carving was a figure, tall and imposing, with eyes that seemed to burn with an inner fire.

"Aakari," Yuna breathed, feeling a shiver run down her spine.

Kael nodded, his expression grim. "This is the story of his imprisonment," he said. "The ancient sorcerers who bound him here were powerful, but they knew that they could not hold him forever. They created a prophecy, one that would determine the fate of the realm."

Yuna felt a surge of excitement mixed with fear. She had always known that she was connected to the prophecy, but she had never imagined that it would be like this.

"What does it say?" she asked, her voice barely above a whisper.

Kael's eyes locked onto hers, his expression serious. "The prophecy says that a descendant of the ancient sorcerers will come, one who possesses the power to either bind Aakari forever or unleash him upon the realm. It is said that this descendant will be born with a mark, a symbol of their power and their destiny."

Yuna felt a shiver run down her spine as she looked down at her hand. On her palm was a small, intricate mark, one that she had always known was special. It was the same mark that was depicted in the carvings on the wall, the same mark that was said to signify the power of the ancient sorcerers.

"I have the mark," she said, her voice barely above a whisper.

Kael's eyes locked onto hers, his expression grim. "Then you are the one," he said. "You are the key to either binding Aakari forever or unleashing him upon the realm."

Yuna felt a surge of fear mixed with determination. She knew that she had a choice to make, one that would determine the fate of the realm. She could bind Aakari, trapping him forever in this prison, or she could unleash him, giving him the power to destroy the realm.

As they stood there, the weight of the prophecy bearing down upon them, Yuna knew that she had to make a decision. She thought of all the people she had met, all the lives that would be affected by her choice. She thought of Kael, of his bravery and his loyalty. And she thought of Aakari, of the power and the danger that he represented.

In the end, it was not a difficult decision. Yuna knew that she could not unleash Aakari upon the realm, not when she had the power to stop him. She reached out, feeling the magic of the ancient sorcerers coursing through her veins.

"I will bind him," she said, her voice firm and resolute. "I will trap him forever in this prison, and I will save the realm from his destruction."

Kael's eyes locked onto hers, his expression grim. "Then let us do it," he said. "Let us bind Aakari and save the realm."

Together, they began the ritual, calling upon the power of the ancient sorcerers to aid them. The magic was powerful, coursing through Yuna's veins like a river of fire. She felt herself being drawn into the ritual, becoming one with the magic and the power of the ancient sorcerers.

As they worked, the air around them began to change. The darkness seemed to recede, pushed back by the light of the magic. The carvings on the wall began to glow, pulsing with a powerful energy. And Yuna felt herself being drawn closer to the heart of the prison, closer to the source of Aakari's power.

Finally, after what seemed like an eternity, the ritual was complete. Yuna felt a surge of power and magic, and she knew that Aakari was bound, trapped forever in this prison. The realm was safe, and Yuna had fulfilled her destiny.

As they stood there, bathed in the glow of the magic, Yuna felt a sense of pride and accomplishment. She had done it, she had saved the realm from destruction. And she knew that she would always stand ready, prepared to defend the realm against any threat that might arise.

But as they turned to leave, Yuna caught a glimpse of something out of the corner of her eye. A figure, tall and imposing, with eyes that seemed to burn with an inner fire. Aakari, the powerful sorcerer, was not as trapped as she had thought.

And Yuna knew that their journey was far from over.

The figure began to move towards them, its eyes fixed on Yuna with an unnerving intensity. Yuna felt a shiver run down her spine as she realized that Aakari was not going to go quietly into the night. He was going to fight, and Yuna was going to have to be ready.

"Kael," she said, her voice low and urgent. "I think we have a problem."

Kael turned, his eyes locking onto the figure. "Aakari," he growled, his hand on the hilt of his sword.

The figure began to move closer, its eyes burning with an inner fire. Yuna felt a surge of magic, and she knew that she was ready. She was ready to face Aakari, to defend the realm against his power.

The battle was intense, with spells and swords clashing in a frenzy of steel and magic. Yuna felt herself being drawn into the fight, her magic and her power rising to meet the challenge. She was a descendant of the ancient sorcerers, and she was not going to back down.

As the fight raged on, Yuna began to feel a sense of unease. Aakari was powerful, more powerful than she had ever imagined. And she was beginning to realize that she might not be able to defeat him, not alone.

But she was not alone. Kael was by her side, his sword flashing in the dim light of the prison. Together, they fought on, their magic and their power combining in a devastating display of steel and sorcery.

And then, just when it seemed like the battle was reaching its climax, everything changed. Aakari stumbled backwards, his eyes widening in surprise. And Yuna saw it, a glimmer of hope in the darkness.

Aakari was not invincible. He had a weakness, a secret that Yuna had uncovered in the ancient texts. And with this knowledge, she knew that she could defeat him, that she could save the realm from his destruction.

With newfound confidence, Yuna launched herself at Aakari, her magic and her power rising to meet the challenge. The battle was fierce, with spells and swords clashing in a frenzy of steel and magic. But Yuna was ready, and she was not going to back down.

In the end, it was Yuna who emerged victorious, her magic and her power proving to be too much for Aakari to handle. The powerful sorcerer stumbled backwards, his eyes widening in defeat. And Yuna stood over him, her chest heaving with exertion, her magic and her power still raging like a storm.

"It's over," she said, her voice firm and resolute. "You will never again threaten the realm."

Aakari looked up at her, his eyes burning with hatred and defeat. "You may have won this battle," he growled, "but the war is far from over. I will return, and next time, you will not be so lucky."

Yuna smiled, a cold and calculating smile. "I'm not lucky," she said. "I'm just better than you. And next time, you will not be so fortunate."

With that, she turned and walked away, leaving Aakari to his fate. The realm was safe, and Yuna had fulfilled her destiny. But she knew that there would be more battles to come, more challenges to face. And she was ready, ready to defend the realm against any threat that might arise.

As they emerged from the prison, Yuna felt a sense of relief wash over her. The battle was won, and the realm was safe. But she knew that there would be more challenges to come, more battles to fight. And she was ready, ready to face whatever the future might hold.

The sun was setting over the forest, casting a golden glow over the trees. Yuna felt a sense of peace wash over her, a sense of closure. She had done it, she had saved the realm from destruction. And she knew that she would always stand ready, prepared to defend the realm against any threat that might arise.

But as they walked away from the prison, Yuna couldn't shake the feeling that they were being watched. She glanced over her shoulder, but there was nothing there. Just the trees, swaying gently in the breeze.

And then, she saw it. A figure, tall and imposing, standing just beyond the treeline. Watching them, waiting for them.

Yuna felt a shiver run down her spine. Who was this figure, and what did they want? She glanced at Kael, but he just shook his head.

"I don't know," he said. "But I think we're about to find out."

The figure began to move towards them, its eyes fixed on Yuna with an unnerving intensity. Yuna felt a surge of magic, and she knew that she was ready. She was ready to face whatever challenges lay ahead, ready to defend the realm against any threat that might arise.

And as the figure drew closer, Yuna saw something that made her heart skip a beat. A mark, a symbol of power and magic. The same mark that she had on her hand, the same mark that signified the power of the ancient sorcerers.

The figure was one of them, a descendant of the ancient sorcerers. And Yuna knew that their journey was far from over. There were more battles to come, more challenges to face. And Yuna was ready, ready to defend the realm against any threat that might arise.

The figure drew closer, its eyes fixed on Yuna with an unnerving intensity. Yuna felt a surge of magic, and she knew that she was ready. She was ready to face whatever challenges lay ahead, ready to defend the realm against any threat that might arise.

"Who are you?" Yuna asked, her voice firm and resolute.

The figure smiled, a cold and calculating smile. "I am one of you," it said. "A descendant of the ancient sorcerers. And I have come to join you on your journey."

Yuna felt a sense of surprise, mixed with a sense of trepidation. What did this figure want, and what did they mean by joining her on her journey? She glanced at Kael, but he just shrugged.

"I think we're about to find out," he said.

The figure began to move closer, its eyes fixed on Yuna with an unnerving intensity. Yuna felt a surge of magic, and she knew that she was ready. She was ready to face whatever challenges lay ahead, ready to defend the realm against any threat that might arise.

And as the figure drew closer, Yuna saw something that made her heart skip a beat. A glimmer of hope, a chance for redemption. The figure was not just a descendant of the ancient sorcerers, but a potential ally. And Yuna knew that she needed all the help she could get.

The battle against Aakari was won, but the war was far from over. There would be more challenges to come, more battles to fight. And Yuna was ready, ready to defend the realm against any threat that might arise.

With the figure by her side, Yuna felt a sense of hope that she had not felt in a long time. Maybe, just maybe, they could defeat the forces of darkness and save the realm from destruction. Maybe, just maybe, they could find a way to bring peace and prosperity to the land.

The journey ahead would be long and difficult, but Yuna was ready. She was ready to face whatever challenges lay ahead, ready to defend the realm against any threat that might arise. And with the figure by her side, she knew that she was not alone.

Together, they would face whatever the future might hold. Together, they would defend the realm against any threat that might arise. And together, they would bring peace and prosperity to the land.

The sun was setting over the forest, casting a golden glow over the trees. Yuna felt a sense of peace wash over her, a sense of closure. She had done it, she had saved the realm from destruction. And she knew that she would always stand ready, prepared to defend the realm against any threat that might arise.

But as they walked away from the prison, Yuna couldn't shake the feeling that they were being watched. She glanced over her shoulder, but there was nothing there. Just the trees, swaying gently in the breeze.

And then, she saw it. A figure, tall and imposing, standing just beyond the treeline. Watching them, waiting for them.

Yuna felt a shiver run down her spine. Who was this figure, and what did they want? She glanced at Kael, but he just shook his head.

"I don't know," he said. "But I think we're about to find out."

The figure began to move towards them, its eyes fixed on Yuna with an unnerving intensity. Yuna felt a surge of magic, and she knew that she was ready. She was ready to face whatever challenges lay ahead, ready to defend the realm against any threat that might arise.

And as the figure drew closer, Yuna saw something that made her heart skip a beat. A mark, a symbol of power and magic. The same mark that she had on her hand, the same mark that signified the power of the ancient sorcerers.

The figure was one of them, a descendant of the ancient sorcerers. And Yuna knew that their journey was far from over. There were more battles to come, more challenges to face. And Yuna was ready, ready to defend the realm against any threat that might arise.

The figure drew closer, its eyes fixed on Yuna with an unnerving intensity. Yuna felt a surge of magic, and she knew that she was ready. She was ready to face whatever challenges lay ahead, ready to defend the realm against any threat that might arise.

"Who are you?" Yuna asked, her voice firm and resolute.

The figure smiled, a cold and calculating smile. "I am one of you," it said. "A descendant of the ancient sorcerers. And I have come to join you on your journey."

Yuna felt a sense of surprise, mixed with a sense of trepidation. What did this figure want, and what did they mean by joining her on her journey? She glanced at Kael, but he just shrugged.

"I think we're about to find out," he said.

The figure began to move closer, its eyes fixed on Yuna with an unnerving intensity. Yuna felt a surge of magic, and she knew that she was ready. She was ready to face whatever challenges lay ahead, ready to defend the realm against any threat that might arise.

And as the figure drew closer, Yuna saw something that made her heart skip a beat. A glimmer of hope, a chance for redemption. The figure was not just a descendant of the ancient sorcerers, but a potential ally. And Yuna knew that she needed all the help she could get.

The battle against Aakari was won, but the war was far from over. There would be more challenges to come, more battles to fight. And Yuna was ready, ready to defend the realm against any threat that might arise.

With the figure by her side, Yuna felt a sense of hope that she had not felt in a long time. Maybe, just maybe, they could defeat the forces of darkness and save the realm from destruction. Maybe, just maybe, they could find a way to bring peace and prosperity to the land.

The journey ahead would be long and difficult, but Yuna was ready. She was ready to face whatever challenges lay ahead, ready to defend the realm against any threat that might arise. And with the figure by her side, she knew that she was not alone.

Together, they would face whatever the future might hold. Together, they would defend the realm against any threat that might arise. And together, they would bring peace and prosperity to the land.

As they walked away from the prison, Yuna felt a sense of hope that she had not felt in a long time. Maybe, just maybe, they

CHAPTER XI

The Darkened Path

The air in the Academy Hall hung thick with disbelief. Yuna's pronouncements, echoing through the cavernous space, had detonated like a carefully placed explosive. Kael, their friend, their comrade, a vital piece of their team... a traitor?

Callum stood frozen, his hand still hovering near the hilt of his sword. His mind struggled to reconcile the Kael he knew – the quick-witted strategist, the loyal friend, the ever-present source of dry humor – with this accusation of treachery. He glanced at Yuna, her face a mask of grim determination, then at Kael, whose expression was a complex tapestry of defiance, guilt, and something else Callum couldn't quite decipher.

The assembled mages, instructors, and students whispered amongst themselves, the murmur growing into a low hum of shock and suspicion. The air crackled with latent magic, a reflection of the volatile emotions swirling within the hall.

"Kael," Yuna said, her voice ringing with a firmness that belied the hurt in her eyes. "Tell me it's not true. Tell me Aakari hasn't poisoned your mind."

Kael remained silent for a long moment, his gaze fixed on the intricate patterns of the floor. The silence stretched, each second amplifying the tension in the room. Finally, he lifted his head, his eyes meeting Yuna's. What Callum saw there confirmed the dread that threatened to consume him.

"It's true," Kael said, the words barely a whisper, yet carrying the weight of a confession. "I... I pledged allegiance to Aakari."

A collective gasp swept through the hall. Master Elmsworth(An elder who protects Eldoria), his face etched with disappointment and disbelief, stepped forward. "Kael... explain yourself. What madness possesses you?"

Kael took a deep breath, the act seeming to steel his resolve. "Madness? No, Master Elmsworth. It's... ambition. An opportunity I couldn't refuse."

"Ambition? At the cost of everything we stand for? At the cost of Eldoria?" Callum finally found his voice, laced with a bitter incredulity. He stepped closer to Kael, his hand now firmly gripping the hilt of his sword. "What could Aakari possibly offer you that would make you betray us all?"

"Power," Kael replied, his voice now stronger, laced with a dangerous edge. "Aakari promised me power beyond my wildest dreams. Power to reshape Eldoria, to cleanse it of the weakness and stagnation that plague it."

"Cleansing Eldoria? You sound just like Aakari!" Yuna retorted, her voice sharp. "His idea of cleansing is to conquer and enslave! Is that what you want?"

"No!" Kael snapped, his eyes flashing. "That's not what I want. I don't want Eldoria enslaved. I want it... better. "

"Better? By serving a tyrant?" Callum scoffed. "You've lost your mind, Kael. You're not the Kael I know."

"Perhaps you never truly knew me, Callum," Kael said, a hint of sadness flickering in his eyes. "Perhaps all of you were too blinded by your own ideals to see what I truly desired. Look at Eldoria. We cling to tradition, to ancient ways, while the world around us evolves. Aakari offers change, a brutal change, perhaps, but a change nonetheless. And I intend to guide that change, to mold it into something..."

"Something better? By helping a man who wants to drown the world in darkness?" Yuna interrupted, her voice ringing with disbelief. "You're deluding yourself, Kael. You're being used."

Kael flinched, a flicker of doubt crossing his face. But he quickly masked it with a renewed defiance. "I am not being used. I am using Aakari. I am playing a longer game than you can possibly comprehend."

Master Elmsworth shook his head sadly. "Kael, you have made a terrible mistake. Aakari is not to be trusted. He will only lead you down a path of destruction."

"I am aware of the risks, Master," Kael said, his voice hardening. "But I am willing to take them. The potential reward is too great."

"And what is this reward, exactly?" Callum pressed, his voice dangerously low. "Enlighten us, Kael. What grand vision justifies your betrayal?"

Kael hesitated, his gaze flickering between Callum and Yuna. He seemed to be weighing his words carefully. Finally, he spoke. "I... I want to rewrite the rules. The balance of power has to shift. The strong should rule, not be held back by the weak. Eldoria needs a strong hand, and Aakari... Aakari can provide that strength."

"And you, of course, see yourself as the guiding hand behind Aakari's strength?" Yuna said, her voice laced with sarcasm.

Kael didn't answer, but the look in his eyes confirmed her suspicion. He truly believed he could control Aakari, that he could use the tyrant's power for his own ends. It was a naive and dangerous delusion.

"Kael, there is still time to turn back," Master Elmsworth pleaded. "Renounce Aakari. Return to us. We can help you find a better path."

"It's too late for that, Master," Kael said, his voice tinged with regret. "I have made my choice."

He reached into his cloak and drew out a small, obsidian-like object. It pulsed with a dark, malevolent energy that made the air around it shimmer.

"This," Kael said, holding the object aloft, "is the key to my power. A gift from Aakari himself. It amplifies my abilities beyond anything I could have imagined."

As soon as Kael showed them what his new master had given to him Yuna and Callum knew who was responsible for the whole situation. Aakari was known for corrupting people and using any method to manipulate them. He was very powerful so it was almost impossible to beat him face to face.

Callum and Yuna exchanged a look. They knew that they were running out of time.

Master Elmsworth gasped. "That... that is a Shadowstone! An artifact of immense dark power! Where did you get that?"

"Aakari gave it to me," Kael said, a strange pride in his voice. "He recognized my potential, my ambition. He saw that I was worthy of wielding such power."

"Worthy?" Yuna scoffed. "He saw that you were easily manipulated. He gave you a Shadowstone to control you, to turn you into his puppet!"

Kael's face darkened. "I am no one's puppet! I control the Shadowstone, it does not control me."

"That's what they all say," Callum said grimly. "But the Shadowstones always corrupt. They amplify your desires, twist your ambitions, and ultimately consume you."

"I am stronger than that," Kael insisted. "I can resist its influence."

"No one can, Kael," Yuna said, her voice softening. "The Shadowstones are inherently corrupting. They feed on your negative emotions, your fears, your insecurities. They amplify your darkest desires until they consume you entirely."

"Enough!" Kael shouted, his voice cracking with anger. "I will not stand here and listen to your lectures. I have made my choice, and I will not be swayed."

He raised the Shadowstone, and the dark energy emanating from it intensified. The air crackled with power, and the ground beneath their feet began to tremble.

"I am going to change Eldoria," Kael declared, his eyes burning with fanaticism. "I am going to make it stronger, more powerful, more... perfect."

"You're going to destroy it," Callum said, his voice cold and hard. "You're going to become a monster, Kael. And we can't let that happen."

He drew his sword, the steel gleaming in the dim light of the Academy Hall. Yuna, her face set in a grim determination, began to chant an incantation, her hands glowing with arcane energy.

"I'm sorry, Kael," Callum said, his voice filled with regret. "But I have to stop you."

"Stop me?" Kael laughed, a harsh, hollow sound. "You can't stop me. I am more powerful than you can possibly imagine."

He unleashed the power of the Shadowstone, and a torrent of dark energy erupted from it, engulfing the hall in a swirling vortex of shadows.

The battle in the Academy Hall had been fierce and destructive. Kael, empowered by the Shadowstone, had proven to be a formidable opponent. He unleashed blasts of dark energy, summoned shadowy constructs, and moved with a speed and agility that defied belief.

Callum and Yuna fought with all their skill and courage, but they were constantly on the defensive. Kael's power was simply overwhelming. They managed to land a few blows, but the Shadowstone seemed to be constantly replenishing Kael's energy, healing his wounds almost instantaneously.

Finally, after what seemed like an eternity, Callum managed to disarm Kael, knocking the Shadowstone from his hand. But as the stone clattered to the floor, a surge of dark energy erupted from it, knocking Callum back against a wall.

Yuna seized the opportunity and launched a powerful spell at Kael, forcing him to stumble. But before she could follow up with another attack, Kael unleashed a wave of dark energy that knocked her off her feet as well.

Both Callum and Yuna lay sprawled on the floor, exhausted and battered. Kael stood over them, the Shadowstone hovering menacingly nearby.

"It's over," Kael said, his voice filled with triumph. "I have won."

He reached out to retrieve the Shadowstone, but as his fingers closed around it, a searing pain shot through his body. He cried out in agony and stumbled back, clutching his hand.

He looked down at his hand and saw that it was covered in black, festering wounds. The Shadowstone was burning his flesh, corrupting him from the inside out.

"What... what's happening?" Kael gasped, his voice filled with fear.

"The Shadowstone is rejecting you," Yuna said, struggling to her feet. "It senses that you're not truly evil, that you still have a shred of goodness left in you."

"But... but Aakari said..." Kael stammered.

"Aakari lied," Callum said, also getting to his feet. "He only wanted to use you, to corrupt you. He doesn't care about you, Kael. He only cares about power."

Kael looked from Callum to Yuna, his face a mask of confusion and despair. He finally understood the truth. He had been used, manipulated, and betrayed by Aakari.

"I... I didn't want this," Kael said, his voice barely a whisper. "I just wanted to make Eldoria better."

"We know, Kael," Yuna said softly. "We know."

Kael looked down at the Shadowstone, his face filled with disgust. He clenched his fist and crushed the stone into dust. The dark energy that had been coursing through him dissipated, and he collapsed to the floor, exhausted and defeated.

Callum and Yuna rushed to his side.

"Are you alright, Kael?" Callum asked, his voice filled with concern.

"I... I don't know," Kael said, his voice weak. "I feel... empty. Like something has been ripped out of me."

"That's the Shadowstone," Yuna said. "It feeds on your soul, slowly draining your life force. But you're free of it now. You'll heal."

They helped Kael to his feet and led him to a nearby bench. He sat down heavily, his head in his hands.

"I'm so sorry," Kael said, his voice filled with remorse. "I betrayed you. I almost destroyed everything."

"It's alright, Kael," Callum said, placing a hand on his shoulder. "We all make mistakes. What matters is that you realized your mistake and corrected it."

"But... can you ever forgive me?" Kael asked, his eyes filled with pleading.

Yuna and Callum exchanged a look. They had both been deeply hurt by Kael's betrayal, but they also knew that he had been manipulated by Aakari. They knew that he still had good in him.

"Yes, Kael," Yuna said, her voice filled with sincerity. "We forgive you."

A wave of relief washed over Kael's face. "Thank you," he said, his voice choked with emotion. "Thank you both."

Callum smiled. "Now, let's figure out how to undo the stupid mess you got us into."

The tension in the air eased, replaced by a fragile sense of hope. The betrayal had been devastating, but it had also revealed the true strength of their friendship. They had faced the darkness and emerged stronger, more united than ever before.

But the victory was bittersweet. They knew that Aakari was still out there, plotting his conquest of Eldoria. And they knew that they had a long and difficult road ahead of them.

The immediate aftermath of Kael's betrayal was a flurry of activity. The Academy' elders who protected Eldoria were placed on high alert. Reinforcements were called in from the surrounding settlements. Master Elmsworth, his face etched with worry, began to coordinate the defenses of the Academy and the surrounding area. (You need to know about the fact that none of the academy's students or teachers knew about this)

Callum and Yuna, despite their exhaustion, threw themselves into the effort. They helped to reinforce the Academy's defenses, trained the younger students in basic combat skills, and assisted Master Elmsworth in planning their next move. Kael, still weak and shaken, remained largely confined to his room. He was consumed by guilt and remorse, struggling to come to terms with the enormity of his betrayal. He spent hours poring over ancient texts, searching for a way to atone for his mistakes.

One evening, Yuna found Kael hunched over a dusty tome, his face illuminated by the flickering light of a candle.

"How are you holding up?" she asked softly, sitting down beside him.

Kael looked up, his eyes red-rimmed and weary. "Not well," he admitted. "I can't shake the feeling that I've irrevocably damaged everything. My reputation, my friendships... everything."

"You made a mistake, Kael," Yuna said, taking his hand. "But you're paying the price for it. You're trying to make amends. That's all that matters."

"But what if it's not enough?" Kael asked, his voice filled with despair. "What if I can never truly redeem myself?"

"Don't say that," Yuna said firmly. "There's always hope for redemption. You just have to keep fighting for it."

She paused, then added, "Besides, we need you, Kael. Your knowledge, your skills... they're invaluable. We can't defeat Aakari without you."

Kael looked at her, a flicker of hope igniting in his eyes. "You really think so?"

"I know so," Yuna said, squeezing his hand. "We're a team, Kael. We need each other. And we're going to face this together."

Kael managed a weak smile. "Thank you, Yuna. You don't know how much that means to me."

"Anytime," Yuna said, returning his smile.

They sat in silence for a few moments, the only sound the crackling of the candle. Finally, Yuna spoke.

"So, what are you reading?" she asked, gesturing to the tome in front of him.

"It's an ancient text on the history of the Shadowstones," Kael said. "I'm trying to figure out where Aakari got it and how he was able to control it."

"And have you found anything?" Yuna asked.

Kael nodded. "I think so. According to this text, the Shadowstones were originally created by a powerful sorcerer named Malkor millennia ago. He sought to harness the power of the shadows to conquer Eldoria, but he was ultimately defeated and his Shadowstones were scattered across the land."

"Scattered, but not destroyed," Yuna said grimly.

"No," Kael said. "And according to this text, the Shadowstones can be found wherever there is great darkness and despair. They feed on negative emotions, growing stronger with each act of violence and hatred."

"So, Aakari must have found a place filled with those very things," Yuna said thoughtfully. "But where?"

Kael shrugged. "I don't know. But this text mentions a specific ritual that Malkor used to create the Shadowstones. It requires a great deal of dark energy and a sacrifice of immense power."

"A sacrifice?" Yuna asked, her eyes widening. "What kind of sacrifice?"

"The text doesn't say," Kael said. "But it implies that it was something terrible, something that shook the very foundations of Eldoria."

Yuna shuddered. "We need to find out more about this ritual," she said. "We need to know what Aakari is planning."

"I agree," Kael said. "But this text is all I have. I don't know where else to look."

"Maybe I can help," Callum said, entering the room. He had overheard their conversation and was intrigued by what they were saying.

"How?" Yuna asked.

"Actually I read about a power source that helps reverse the negativity of the shadow stone, so we need not do any sacrifice" Callum said taking out a thick book on moon crystals the Volume- ii from his bag. And starts reading through the middle page of it.

" I am such stupid not to ask you Callum cause i forgot you have read the most books among us." said Kael smiling

"Is there any ritual saying that we could create Shadow stones " asked Yuna crossing her fingers as she saw her Callum flip through the pages of the dusty thick book.

"Here, it says take a small circular moon crystal and melt it and a pinch of moon dust , but here is something written in a language i don't know it is written you have to sacrifise the and then the language is changed." Said Callum with a calm look on his face as he did not want anyone to fall for the shadow stone again.

" And i guess we are the lucky ones, cause i know that it would be better for us not to make them" said Kael with a weired expression on his face which i guess i cannot explain..

Then the trio laughed looking at Kael and from there, they told that they would remain friend atleast for some decades and went to there Alchemy classes on that saturday afternoon. There exams were close so they needed attendence. (this book will not mention much about there studies as i think they might bore you out soo.... we will talk about the adventures they had)

CHAPTER XII

Confronting the Shadows

Yuna stood before the Council of Elders, her heart pounding with anticipation and a hint of fear. The weight of her newfound destiny settled upon her like a mantle, and she felt the burden of responsibility acutely. The elders, wise and venerable, gazed at her with knowing eyes, their faces etched with the lines of time and experience.

"Yuna, child of the royal blood," began Elder Arin, his voice low and soothing, "we have come to understand the truth about your heritage and the prophecy that surrounds you. You are the chosen one, the warrior-queen destined to save our world from the darkness that threatens to consume it."

Yuna felt a shiver run down her spine as the elder's words echoed through the chamber. She had always known that she was different, that she possessed a unique energy and strength that set her apart from others. But to hear it spoken aloud, to have her suspicions confirmed, was both exhilarating and terrifying.

"Aakari, the dark sorcerer, seeks to return to power," continued Elder Arin, his eyes clouding with concern. "He will stop at nothing to claim the throne and destroy all that is good in our world. You, Yuna, are the only one who can prevent this catastrophe."

Yuna felt a surge of determination course through her veins. She was ready to face whatever challenges lay ahead, to confront the shadows that had haunted her for so long. But she knew that she could not do it alone.

"What can I do?" she asked, her voice firm and resolute. "How can I stop Aakari and fulfill my destiny?"

The elders exchanged glances, their faces grave with the weight of their knowledge. "We have devised a plan," said Elder Lirien, her voice soft and melodious. "But it will require great courage and cunning. You must journey to the heart of the dark sorcerer's stronghold, gather allies and resources, and prepare for the final battle."

Yuna's heart skipped a beat as she listened to the elder's words. She had never been one to shy away from danger, but the thought of facing Aakari and his minions was daunting, to say the least. Yet, she steeled herself, drawing upon the inner reserves of strength and courage that had always defined her.

"I am ready," she said, her voice firm and resolute. "I will not falter or fail. I will do whatever it takes to save our world and fulfill my destiny."

The elders nodded, their faces set with determination. "Then let us begin," said Elder Arin, his voice low and urgent. "The fate of our world hangs in the balance, and time is running out. We must act swiftly and decisively, or risk losing everything that we hold dear."

Together, Yuna and the elders pored over ancient tomes and scrolls, seeking out the secrets of the dark sorcerer's power and the weaknesses that could be exploited. They spoke of magic and strategy, of alliances and battles, and of the ultimate showdown between light and darkness.

As the night wore on, Yuna felt her mind expanding, her horizons broadening. She was no longer just a young warrior, trained in the art of combat and magic. She was a leader, a queen, a symbol of hope in a world torn apart by darkness and despair.

And with this realization, Yuna felt a sense of peace settle upon her. She knew that she was exactly where she was meant to be, that she was fulfilling her destiny and living up to her true potential. The shadows that had haunted her for so long began to recede, replaced by a sense of purpose and direction.

As the first light of dawn crept over the horizon, Yuna rose from her seat, her eyes shining with a newfound sense of determination. "I am ready," she said, her voice firm and resolute. "I will face whatever challenges lie ahead, and I will emerge victorious. For I am Yuna, the warrior-queen, and I will not be defeated."

The elders nodded, their faces set with approval. "Then go, Yuna," said Elder Arin, his voice low and urgent. "Go and fulfill your destiny. The fate of our world depends on it."

With a sense of purpose and direction, Yuna set out on her journey, ready to face whatever challenges lay ahead. She knew that the road would be long and difficult, that she would face countless dangers and uncertainties. But she was undaunted, for she knew that she was not alone.

She had the support of the elders, the wisdom of the ancient tomes, and the power of her own inner strength. And with these allies by her side, Yuna felt invincible, ready to take on the darkness and emerge victorious.

As she walked, the sun rising over the horizon, Yuna felt a sense of joy and freedom that she had never known before. She was no longer just a young warrior, bound by the constraints of her past. She was a queen, a leader, a symbol of hope in a world torn apart by darkness and despair.

And with this realization, Yuna felt her heart soar, her spirit lifting on the winds of change. She knew that she would face many challenges, that the road ahead would be long and difficult. But she was ready, for she knew that she was exactly where she was meant to be.

The journey was just beginning, and Yuna was eager to see what lay ahead. She knew that she would face many dangers, that she would be tested and tried in ways that she could hardly imagine. But she was undaunted, for she knew that she was strong, that she was capable of overcoming any obstacle.

And so, with a sense of purpose and direction, Yuna set out on her journey, ready to face whatever challenges lay ahead. She knew that the fate of her world depended on it, and she was determined to do whatever it took to save it.

As she walked, the sun rising over the horizon, Yuna felt a sense of peace settle upon her. She knew that she was exactly where she was meant to be, that she was fulfilling her destiny and living up to her true potential. The shadows that had haunted her for so long began to recede, replaced by a sense of purpose and direction.

And with this realization, Yuna felt her heart soar, her spirit lifting on the winds of change. She knew that she would face many challenges, that the road ahead would be long and difficult. But she was ready, for she knew that she was strong, that she was capable of overcoming any obstacle.

The journey was just beginning, and Yuna was eager to see what lay ahead. She knew that she would face many dangers, that she would be tested and tried in ways that she could hardly imagine. But she was undaunted, for she knew that she was not alone.

She had the support of the elders, the wisdom of the ancient tomes, and the power of her own inner strength. And with these allies by her side, Yuna felt invincible, ready to take on the darkness and emerge victorious.

As the sun rose higher in the sky, Yuna came to a great forest, its trees towering above her like giants. She knew that this was the first challenge, the first test of her courage and strength. For in the heart of the forest, there lived a fearsome beast, a creature of legend and myth.

The beast was said to be fierce and terrifying, with scales as black as coal and eyes that glowed like embers. It was said to be able to breathe fire, to destroy anything that stood in its way. And Yuna knew that she would have to face it, to defeat it if she was to succeed in her quest.

But she was not afraid, for she knew that she was strong. She had the power of the ancient magic, the wisdom of the elders, and the courage of her own heart. And with these allies by her side, Yuna felt invincible, ready to take on the beast and emerge victorious.

As she walked through the forest, the trees growing taller and closer together, Yuna felt a sense of excitement and anticipation. She knew that the beast was near, that she could feel its presence, its power. And she steeled herself, drawing upon the inner reserves of strength and courage that had always defined her.

The beast emerged from the shadows, its eyes glowing like embers in the dark. Yuna stood tall, her heart pounding with excitement and fear. She knew that this was the moment, the moment of truth. And she was ready, for she knew that she was strong, that she was capable of overcoming any obstacle.

The battle was fierce and intense, the beast breathing fire and destruction. But Yuna was undaunted, for she knew that she had the power of the ancient magic, the wisdom of the elders, and the courage of her own heart. And with these allies by her side, she fought with all her might, using every trick and tactic that she knew.

In the end, it was Yuna who emerged victorious, the beast defeated and destroyed. And as she stood tall, her chest heaving with exhaustion, Yuna felt a sense of pride and accomplishment. She had faced her fears, and she had emerged victorious.

The journey was far from over, but Yuna knew that she was ready. She had faced the first challenge, and she had succeeded. And she knew that she would face many more, that the road ahead would be long and difficult. But she was undaunted, for she knew that she was strong, that she was capable of overcoming any obstacle.

As she walked through the forest, the sun setting over the horizon, Yuna felt a sense of peace settle upon her. She knew that she was exactly where she was meant to be, that she was fulfilling her destiny and living up to her true potential. The shadows that had haunted her for so long began to recede, replaced by a sense of purpose and direction.

And with this realization, Yuna felt her heart soar, her spirit lifting on the winds of change. She knew that she would face many challenges, that the road ahead would be long and difficult. But she was ready, for she knew that she was not alone.

She had the support of the elders, the wisdom of the ancient tomes, and the power of her own inner strength. And with these allies by her side, Yuna felt invincible, ready to take on the darkness and emerge victorious.

The journey was just beginning, and Yuna was eager to see what lay ahead. She knew that she would face many dangers, that she would be tested and tried in ways that she could hardly imagine. But she was undaunted, for she knew that she was strong, that she was capable of overcoming any obstacle.

And so, with a sense of purpose and direction, Yuna set out on her journey, ready to face whatever challenges lay ahead. She knew that the fate of her world depended on it, and she was determined to do whatever it took to save it.

As the sun dipped below the horizon, Yuna came to a great mountain, its peak towering above her like a giant. She knew that this was the next challenge, the next test of her courage and strength. For in the heart of the mountain, there lived a powerful sorceress, a woman of great wisdom and knowledge.

The sorceress was said to be able to see into the hearts of those who sought her out, to know their deepest desires and fears. And Yuna knew that she would have to face her, to seek out her wisdom and guidance. For the sorceress was the only one who could help her unlock the secrets of the ancient magic, to understand the true nature of her power.

But Yuna was not afraid, for she knew that she was strong. She had the power of the ancient magic, the wisdom of the elders, and the courage of her own heart. And with these allies by her side, Yuna felt invincible, ready to take on the sorceress and emerge victorious.

As she climbed the mountain, the air growing thinner and colder, Yuna felt a sense of excitement and anticipation. She knew that the sorceress was near, that she could feel her presence, her power. And she steeled herself, drawing upon the inner reserves of strength and courage that had always defined her.

The sorceress emerged from the shadows, her eyes gleaming with wisdom and knowledge. Yuna stood tall, her heart pounding with excitement and fear. She knew that this was the moment, the moment of truth. And she was ready, for she knew that she was strong, that she was capable of overcoming any obstacle.

The sorceress gazed into Yuna's heart, seeing her deepest desires and fears. And Yuna felt a sense of vulnerability, of exposure. But she was not afraid, for she knew that she was strong. She had the power of the ancient magic, the wisdom of the elders, and the courage of her own heart. And with these allies by her side, Yuna felt invincible, ready to take on the sorceress and emerge victorious.

The sorceress spoke, her voice low and melodious. "Yuna, child of the royal blood," she said, "I see that you are strong, that you are capable of overcoming any obstacle. But I also see that you are afraid, that you are uncertain of your destiny."

Yuna felt a sense of surprise, of wonder. How did the sorceress know these things? But she was not afraid, for she knew that she was strong. She had the power of the ancient magic, the wisdom of the elders, and the courage of her own heart. And with these allies by her side, Yuna felt invincible, ready to take on the sorceress and emerge victorious.

"I am afraid," Yuna said, her voice firm and resolute. "But I am not uncertain of my destiny. I know that I am meant to save my world, to defeat the darkness and bring light to those who dwell in shadow."

The sorceress nodded, her eyes gleaming with wisdom and knowledge. "Then you are indeed strong," she said. "For you have faced your fears, and you have emerged victorious. And now, I will give you the gift of my wisdom, the gift of my knowledge."

And with that, the sorceress reached out and touched Yuna's forehead. Yuna felt a surge of energy, a flood of knowledge and wisdom. She saw the secrets of the ancient magic, the true nature of her power. And she knew that she was ready, that she was prepared to face whatever challenges lay ahead.

The journey was far from over, but Yuna knew that she was ready. She had faced the first two challenges, and she had succeeded. And she knew that she would face many more, that the road ahead would be long and difficult. But she was undaunted, for she knew that she was strong, that she was capable of overcoming any obstacle.

As she walked down the mountain, the sun rising over the horizon, Yuna felt a sense of peace settle upon her. She knew that she was exactly where she was meant to be, that she was fulfilling her destiny and living up to her true potential. The shadows that had haunted her for so long began to recede, replaced by a sense of purpose and direction.

And with this realization, Yuna felt her heart soar, her spirit lifting on the winds of change. She knew that she would face many challenges, that the road ahead would be long and difficult. But she was ready, for she knew that she was not alone.

She had the support of the elders, the wisdom of the ancient tomes, and the power of her own inner strength. And with these allies by her side, Yuna felt invincible, ready to take on the darkness and emerge victorious.

The journey was just beginning, and Yuna was eager to see what lay ahead. She knew that she would face many dangers, that she would be tested and tried in ways that she could hardly imagine. But she was undaunted, for she knew that she was strong, that she was capable of overcoming any obstacle.

And so, with a sense of purpose and direction, Yuna set out on her journey, ready to face whatever challenges lay ahead. She knew that the fate of her world depended on it, and she was determined to do whatever it took to save it.

As the sun rose higher in the sky, Yuna came to a great river, its waters flowing like a mighty serpent. She knew that this was the next challenge, the next test of her courage and strength. For in the heart of the river, there lived a powerful water spirit, a being of great wisdom and knowledge.

The water spirit was said to be able to control the waters, to summon great waves and whirlpools. And Yuna knew that she would have to face her, to seek out her wisdom and guidance. For the water spirit was the only one who could help her unlock the secrets of the ancient magic, to understand the true nature of her power.

But Yuna was not afraid, for she knew that she was strong. She had the power of the ancient magic, the wisdom of the elders, and the courage of her own heart. And with these allies by her side, Yuna felt invincible, ready to take on the water spirit and emerge victorious.

As she walked along the river, the water flowing like a mighty serpent, Yuna felt a sense of excitement and anticipation. She knew that the water spirit was near, that she could feel her presence, her power. And she steeled herself, drawing upon the inner reserves of strength and courage that had always defined her.

The water spirit emerged from the depths, her eyes gleaming with wisdom and knowledge. Yuna stood tall, her heart pounding with excitement and fear. She knew that this was the moment, the moment of truth. And she was ready, for she knew that she was strong, that she was capable of overcoming any obstacle.

The water spirit spoke, her voice low and melodious. "Yuna, child of the royal blood," she said, "I see that you are strong, that you are capable of overcoming any obstacle. But I also see that you are uncertain, that you are unsure of your destiny."

Yuna felt a sense of surprise, of wonder. How did the water spirit know these things? But she was not afraid, for she knew that she was strong. She had the power of the ancient magic, the wisdom of the elders, and the courage of her own heart. And with these allies by her side, Yuna felt invincible, ready to take on the water spirit and emerge victorious.

"I am uncertain," Yuna said, her voice firm and resolute. "But I am not unsure of my destiny. I know that I am meant to save my world, to defeat the darkness and bring light to those who dwell in shadow."

The water spirit nodded, her eyes gleaming with wisdom and knowledge. "Then you are indeed strong," she said. "For you have

faced your fears, and you have emerged victorious. And now, I will give you the gift of my wisdom, the gift of my knowledge."
  And

CHAPTER XIII

The Power of Friendship

The air in the hidden grotto hummed not with menace, but with a nascent energy. The fear they had all carried, the heavy cloak of dread that had clung to them since the Shadow War's brutal incursion, was beginning to fray at the edges. It wasn't gone entirely, not by a long shot, but a subtle shift had occurred, a trembling seed of hope planted in the fertile soil of their shared resilience. Yuna sat cross-legged on the cool stone floor, her fingers tracing the worn symbols on the ancient tome they'd unearthed within the grotto's depths. The book, bound in leather as dark and weathered as the cliff face outside, pulsed with a faint warmth, as if a slumbering heart had been nudged awake. It was a grimoire unlike any she'd ever encountered, its pages filled not with rigid spells and incantations, but with stories, allegories, and philosophical musings on the true nature of magic. Across from her, Kael practiced his sword forms, the silver blade reflecting the soft glow of the luminescent moss that clung to the cave walls. His movements were more fluid than before, each parry and thrust imbued with a newfound confidence. He no longer hesitated, no longer flinched at the memory of the shadows that had consumed his home. He was still the same Kael, the boy with the compassionate heart and unwavering loyalty, but he was also something more - a warrior, tempered by loss, steeled by the unwavering faith he placed in his friends. Callum, meanwhile, was perched precariously on a rocky outcrop overlooking the small pool of water at the grotto's center. He wasn't staring aimlessly. He was intensely focused, his brow furrowed as he manipulated the water with subtle gestures of his hands. Small whirlpools swirled and danced before him, coalescing into miniature waves before dissolving back into the tranquil surface. The boy who had once struggled to summon even a flicker of flame was now commanding the very essence of his elemental affinity with a growing precision. The quiet concentration was occasionally punctuated by a soft sigh from Kael's practice, or a contented hum from Callum as he adjusted the water. Yuna, occasionally, mumbled a phrase or two from the grimoire. It was a peaceful tableau, a stark contrast to the chaos that had engulfed their world. But beneath the surface calm, an undeniable current of change was brewing.

"This book... it's not like any other," Yuna finally said, breaking the silence. She looked up at her friends, her emerald eyes shining with a mixture of awe and determination. "It talks about magic as a kind of... symbiotic relationship. It's not just about wielding raw power; it's about understanding the interconnectedness of all things."

Kael sheathed his sword, the sound echoing gently in the grotto. He strode over and sat beside Yuna, his gaze fixed on the ancient book. "What do you mean, interconnectedness?"

Yuna turned a page, her finger tracing a passage illustrated with a depiction of interconnected roots spreading through the soil. "It says that true magic stems from the depths of our own connection to the world, and to each other. That the strongest bonds are not forged in blood, but in empathy, understanding, and shared experience." She looked at Kael with warm eyes. "Like us, right? The bond we share has kept us going."

Callum slid off his perch and joined them, his wet hands leaving damp trails on the stone. "So it's not just about spells and chants?" he asked, a flicker of curiosity brightening his usual solemn expression.

"Not entirely. The book implies that spells are just tools, catalysts for the magic that already resides within us. But to unlock that inner power, it says we must first embrace our connections. The bonds we share amplify our own abilities...or, sometimes, they limit them," Yuna explained, her voice laced with a newfound conviction.

Kael nodded slowly, the implications of her words settling in his mind like a stone. He glanced at Callum, then back at Yuna, finally understanding the shift in energy he'd felt. "So... when we work together, we're not just three individuals, we're... more?"

"Exactly!" Yuna smiled. It was the first genuinely happy smile they had seen in days. "We're a nexus, a point of convergence where our individual strengths combine and resonate. The book calls it a 'Concordance of Souls.'" She ran her hand lovingly over the cover. "It says that when people share a genuine bond, their magic becomes more potent, more resilient."

Callum looked at his hands, the water droplets still clinging to his skin. He had always felt a loneliness, even before the Shadow War. He had always felt like he was outside, looking in, trying to understand why he had been given the magic he had and why his parents had died so young. He had always felt like he was meant to be alone. He had never known the power that comes from being connected to others, like Kayle and Yuna were.

"So... if that's true..." Callum said slowly, his voice barely above a whisper, "then why haven't we felt it before? Why were we struggling so much?"

Yuna turned the page again, pointing to a passage decorated with drawings of intertwined vines, twisted and broken. "Because our connections were weak. We had a bond, yes, but it was fragile, untested. It required the crucible of the Shadow War, the shared trauma and struggle, to truly forge it into something unbreakable."

"So, all the fear, all the loss... it made us stronger?" Kael asked. He had been so angry, so bitter, about what they had lost. He had assumed the only thing that would come out of those losses was more pain. To learn that good could come from even the worst things... it gave him a spark of hope.

"That's the paradox of it," Yuna said, her voice full of warmth. "The darkest moments have the potential to illuminate the greatest strengths. Every time we helped each other, every time we pushed someone out of the way of danger, every time we took that leap of faith and relied on the other, we were reinforcing our bond, making it more resilient. It's not about being fearless or immune to pain; it's about facing the darkness together and knowing that we are not alone."

Kael, never one for flowery language, simply nodded again. The idea settled in the depths of his soul. It wasn't a magic trick, it was a truth buried with his heart and they'd all been too distracted to see it.

Callum looked from Yuna to Kael, a curious, hesitant smile tugging at the corners of his lips. He reached out, placing his hand on Kael's arm. Kael responded by gently taking his hand into his own. Yuna placed her hand on Callum's other arm, creating a triangular bond between them.

A warm, tingling sensation flowed through him, a gentle energy coursing along his skin. It wasn't the same surge of power he felt when he summoned the water, it was something deeper, more resonant. It felt like... home. A place of belonging, of being understood without the need for words. He noticed the other two felt the same warmth and looked back at him.

"What was that?" Callum asked, his voice full of wonder.

"That's the resonance," Yuna whispered, her eyes shining. "That's the energy of our Concordance. It's not just a theory, Callum, it's real."

Kael tested the bond, sending small sparks of energy through his fingers in tune with his emotions. He felt a warmth from Yuna's energy, followed by a gentle chill from Callum's. The emotions weren't physical, but spiritual, and he felt their feelings as clearly as if they were his own.

They sat in silence for a moment, basking in the newfound connection. It was a peaceful moment, a stark contrast to the turmoil that had defined their lives for so long. But this peace felt different, not like a fragile truce born of exhaustion, but rather a deep, abiding calm that had blossomed from within.

The grimoire, Yuna realized, wasn't just about the how of magic; it was about the why. It wasn't about mastering spells, it was about mastering themselves and harnessing the power of human connection.

"We need to learn more," Yuna said, her voice filled with a new sense of purpose. "There's much more to this than just feeling each other's feelings."

Kael nodded, his hand still entwined with Callum's. "We need to learn how to use this. To channel our bond into our magic."

Callum, now feeling the confidence of being included in the group, straightened his back. "If our strength is in our partnership, then we need to learn to fight as one. As a team, not three separate individuals."

The three of them began to pore over the grimoire, the luminescent moss illuminating the ancient script. They spent hours together, delving into the intricate diagrams and philosophical texts, learning about the different ways they could harness their connection. Days turned into weeks, and the hidden grotto became their sanctuary, a place of learning, growth and discovery.

Yuna, guided by the ancient text, discovered that each of them possessed a unique aspect of the Concordance. Yuna was the anchor, the heart that held them together, her power stemming from her empathy and understanding. Kael was the conduit, the channel through which the flow of energy between them was directed. Callum was the catalyst, the spark that ignited their combined power, his elemental affinity amplifying the raw potential of their connection.

They practiced relentlessly, pushing their limits, testing their boundaries, and learning from their failures. Under Yuna's guidance, they practiced their magic in unison. Kael learned to channel his sword strikes with the energy of their bond, his attacks becoming faster and more devastating. Callum discovered how to infuse his water manipulation with their combined power, creating powerful waves and currents that could overwhelm their opponents. Yuna learned to draw upon their emotional connection to amplify her spells, creating protective shields and powerful bursts of energy.

They didn't just practice combat. They worked on their communication. They learned each other's rhythms, their strengths and weaknesses, their triggers and fears. They learned to trust each other implicitly, to anticipate each other's moves, to fight not merely side-by-side, but as a single, harmonious entity.

They laughed, they argued, they cried, but through it all, their bond grew stronger, their connection deeper. They had faced the darkest moments together, and they had emerged, not broken, but reforged like the finest steel.

One evening, as they rested after a particularly strenuous training session, Callum spoke. "I never thought, before all of this, that I'd be this close to anyone. I..." He struggled with the words, trying to explain the emotions that swirled inside of his heart, "I always thought I was meant to be alone."

Kael placed a reassuring hand on Callum's shoulder, his eyes reflecting the same understanding Callum felt. "We all thought that, in our own ways," said Kael. "But look at us now – we're not alone, and we're stronger together than we ever could have been apart."

Yuna smiled, nodding in agreement. "The Shadow War tried to break us, to isolate us, but it failed. It brought us together instead. And it showed us the true power of friendship."

They exchanged a look, each feeling the strength of the bond that bound them. They weren't just friends; they were family, allies, and more importantly, they were a team. They were a force to be reckoned with, not just because of the magic they wielded, but because of the unbreakable bond they shared.

The training hadn't just been about combat and magic, it was about trust and empathy. It meant being in tune with the other's feelings and reactions. It was about being able to anticipate each other's needs without a single word being said. They were a team, and they were ready to fight.

With their training complete, they knew the time for hiding was over. They could no longer stand by while the darkness consumed everything they held dear. They had to face their fears, confront the shadows that had taken their homes and the lives of the people they loved.

The time for the ultimate battle was drawing near. They felt it in the air, in the subtle shift in the flow of magic around them. They knew that their enemy, whoever it may be, would not wait forever. They needed to prepare themselves, not just physically and magically, but mentally and emotionally as well. Yuna pulled them into a circle, placing her hands on top of theirs as they moved to face each other. All three of them felt the power, the energy, and the love that bound them. "We face the darkness as one. We will fight as a single unit, and we will defeat whoever dares stand in our way. I know in my heart that we can do this."

Kael nodded, his resolve strengthened by the bond he shared with his friends. "We'll do this together, Yuna. We always have." Callum squeezed the hands of his friends, his voice filled with a sense of belonging for the first time. "We are the Concordance of Souls. And we are ready." Their eyes met, a spark of determination igniting in each of their hearts. They were ready. They were stronger than ever before. They were the embodiment of the power of friendship, and they would face the coming battle as one. They would face it together, united by an unbreakable bond of love, trust, and unwavering loyalty. The very air pulsed with the promise of the coming storm, but within the grotto, a new kind of power radiated out: the light of unbreakable friendship. It was a beacon of hope, a testament to the strength that could be found not in isolation, but in connection, a power that could rival any darkness. And it was the power that would, they knew, lead them to victory.

CHAPTER XIV

A Royal Legacy

The weight of the revelation pressed on Yuna, a heavy cloak woven from centuries of secrets. Three days. Three days until the Arithmetic Exam, the culmination of years of study, and now, overshadowed by the seismic shift in her understanding of herself. Royal blood. Descendant of the Elders. Guardian. Words that seemed impossibly large, impossibly distant, now thrumming within her very being.

Before, she had been Yuna, the quiet student, the diligent learner, the girl who excelled in arcane theory and struggled with practical application. She had been the outsider, the one who always felt a step behind, a whisper away from truly belonging. Now, everything was different. The foundations of her identity had been ripped up, revealing roots that stretched back to the very dawn of the academy, to the mages who had first harnessed the raw power of Arithmancy and woven it into the fabric of their world.

It wasn't just information; it was a feeling. A deep resonance within her soul, as though a long-dormant chord had finally been struck, vibrating with an ancient power. She felt... different. More grounded, more sure. As if the pieces of a puzzle, scattered and confusing for so long, had finally snapped into place.

The discovery had unfolded in the ancient library, a hushed sanctuary filled with the scent of aged parchment and whispered secrets. Elara, her mentor, had carefully guided her through crumbling texts and forgotten genealogies, her voice a reverent murmur as she unveiled the truth. Yuna had listened, numb at first, then increasingly awestruck, the implications of each revealed connection cascading over her like a waterfall.

She was a descendant of the Eldest, the twelve original mages who had founded the academy, each a master of a specific arcane discipline. Her bloodline traced back to the Arithmancer of Numbers, whose mastery had shaped the very architecture of reality. But more than that, she was a guardian, a protector of the balance, destined to wield a power far beyond the comprehension of ordinary mages. And she had to do all this while keeping her true identity a secret from the entire Academy.

The knowledge had been a gift, but also a burden. A gift of understanding, of purpose, but a burden of responsibility that threatened to crush her. The weight of expectations, the potential dangers, the inherent loneliness of her destiny – they all loomed large in her mind.

But amidst the turmoil, a strange sense of peace had begun to settle within her. She was no longer just Yuna, the ordinary student. She was part of something bigger, something ancient, something vital. And with that realization came a newfound confidence, a quiet strength that she hadn't known she possessed.

She looked at herself in the simple mirror of her dorm room. The same face stared back, framed by dark, unruly hair. The same intelligent, slightly apprehensive eyes. But something had changed. There was a flicker of something...fiercer...in her gaze. A quiet determination.

The key, Elara had emphasized, was balance. She had to prepare for the Arithmetic Exam, to prove her academic merit, to blend in with the other students. She couldn't afford to draw attention to herself, to arouse suspicion. If her true identity were revealed prematurely, it could jeopardize everything. The prophecies, the ancient wards protecting the academy, even the fragile peace of the magical world.

So, Yuna had to be two people. Yuna the student, striving for excellence, and Yuna the guardian, quietly preparing for a destiny she barely understood. It was a delicate dance, a dangerous game of deception. And she had to start playing it now.

The first step was to focus on the exam. To bury herself in equations and theorems, to let the familiar logic of Arithmancy soothe the turbulent waters of her mind. She pulled out her textbooks, her notes, her meticulously organized scrolls. The symbols and formulas, once daunting and intimidating, now seemed to resonate with a deeper meaning. She saw patterns she hadn't noticed before, connections that had previously eluded her.

She attacked the problems with a newfound intensity, her mind racing, her quill flying across the parchment. The numbers seemed to sing to her, to whisper their secrets. She felt a connection to them, a kinship that went beyond mere understanding. It was as if the ancient Arithmancer within her bloodline was guiding her hand, illuminating her mind.

She practiced complex calculations, visualizing the flow of magical energy, the intricate interplay of numerical forces. She worked on spatial equations, conjuring three-dimensional projections in her mind's eye, manipulating them with effortless precision. She studied probability theory, predicting the outcomes of arcane rituals, anticipating the unpredictable fluctuations of elemental energies.

She remembered Master Elmsworth's words: "Arithmancy isn't just about numbers, Yuna. It's about understanding the underlying structure of reality. It's about harnessing the power of order to shape chaos. It's about weaving the threads of fate itself."

And now, she understood. She felt the truth of those words reverberating within her. She wasn't just learning equations; she was learning to control the very fabric of existence.

But the knowledge of her heritage, the burgeoning power within her, also presented a challenge. How much to reveal? How to use her abilities without betraying her secret? She had to carefully calibrate her performance on the exam, to demonstrate her skill without raising eyebrows, without appearing too extraordinary.

She decided to err on the side of caution. She would aim for excellence, but not brilliance. She would solve the problems accurately, but not spectacularly. She would demonstrate her understanding, but not her full potential.

It was a frustrating compromise, a stifling restriction on her newfound abilities. But it was necessary. The stakes were too high to risk exposure.

During the breaks from studying, Yuna found herself drawn to the academy gardens, a tranquil oasis of greenery and blossoming flowers. She sought solace in the quiet beauty of nature, allowing the gentle breeze to soothe her mind and the scent of the flowers to calm her nerves.

She wandered through the winding paths, observing the meticulous arrangements of plants, the carefully calibrated balance of colors and textures. Even in the gardens, she saw the underlying principles of Arithmancy at work. The Fibonacci sequence in the spiral arrangement of petals, the golden ratio in the proportions of leaves and branches, the geometric patterns in the honeycomb of a beehive.

The world around her was a symphony of numbers, a testament to the inherent order of the universe. And she, a descendant of the Arithmancers, was uniquely positioned to understand its language, to decipher its secrets.

As she walked, she couldn't help but notice the other students, preparing for the exam in their own ways. Some were huddled in groups, debating theories and exchanging notes. Others were practicing spells, their wands flashing with arcane energy. Still others were simply pacing nervously, their faces etched with anxiety.

None of them suspected the truth about her. To them, she was just Yuna, the quiet girl who always sat in the back of the classroom. The ordinary student, the unassuming learner.

She watched them with a mixture of pity and affection. They were so focused on the immediate challenge of the exam, so oblivious to the larger forces at play. They didn't know that the very future of the academy, the very fate of the magical world, might rest on her shoulders.

The isolation was almost unbearable. She longed to confide in someone, to share the burden of her secret. But she knew she couldn't. The less people knew, the safer she would be. And the Academy.

She thought of her friends, Callum and Kael. They had been her constant companions, her support system, throughout her years at the academy. They had shared her triumphs and her failures, her joys and her sorrows.

She missed their laughter, their camaraderie, their unwavering belief in her. But she couldn't risk involving them in her secret. It would be too dangerous.

She imagined telling them the truth, watching their faces as they struggled to comprehend the magnitude of her revelation. She imagined the fear, the confusion, the potential betrayal.

No. It was better to keep them in the dark, to protect them from the storm that was brewing.

But the silence weighed on her, a heavy shroud that threatened to suffocate her. She needed to vent, to scream, to release the pressure that was building inside her.

So, she turned to the one place where she could truly be herself, where she could express her emotions without fear of judgment or exposure: the practice chambers.

The practice chambers were located deep beneath the academy, a labyrinthine network of rooms and corridors designed for honing magical skills. They were shielded from prying eyes and equipped with advanced wards to contain any wayward spells.

Yuna knew the chambers well. She had spent countless hours there, perfecting her spells, mastering her techniques, pushing her limits. It was her sanctuary, her refuge.

She entered one of the smaller chambers, a simple room with bare stone walls and a single practice dummy in the center. She closed the door behind her, sealing herself off from the outside world.

And then, she unleashed her power.

She focused her mind, channeling the energy that surged within her, the ancient power that flowed through her veins. She summoned her magic, letting it erupt from her like a volcano.

Spells flew from her fingertips, bolts of pure energy that crackled and illuminated the chamber. She manipulated the elements, conjuring flames that danced and swayed, summoning winds that howled and raged, creating illusions that shimmered and distorted reality.

She fought the practice dummy with a ferocity she hadn't known she possessed, unleashing a torrent of spells that tore it apart, reducing it to splinters and dust.

She screamed and raged, letting out all the frustration, the fear, the loneliness that had been building inside her. She pushed herself to the limit, testing her boundaries, exploring the depths of her power.

And as she fought, as she unleashed her magic, she felt a sense of release, a cathartic purging of the emotions that threatened to overwhelm her.

She was no longer just Yuna, the ordinary student. She was the guardian, the descendant of the Elders, the wielder of ancient power.

And she was ready.

Late into the second night, while most of the academy slept, Yuna found herself drawn back to the library. The vast room, usually bustling during the day, was now eerily silent, illuminated only by the soft glow of enchanted braziers. She moved through the towering shelves, her fingers trailing along the spines of ancient tomes, a sense of reverence washing over her.

She wasn't there to study for the Arithmetic Exam. She had already done all she could in that regard, finding a strange comfort in the logical precision of numbers amidst the chaotic swirl of her new reality. No, she was there seeking something else, something deeper. She needed to understand more about her ancestors, about the legacy she was now bound to.

She found her way to a secluded alcove, a hidden corner she had discovered weeks ago during a late-night study session. It housed a collection of texts deemed too delicate for general circulation, books bound in dragonhide and clasped with enchanted silver. Master Elara had granted her special access, knowing her dedication to research.

Tonight, however, her focus wasn't on academic pursuits. She was searching for any mention of the guardians, any clues about their role, their responsibilities, their powers. The texts were frustratingly vague, filled with cryptic prophecies and symbolic imagery.

She found one passage, hidden within a commentary on the Arithmancy of Celestial Bodies, that caught her attention. It spoke of a "blood of the Elders," a lineage destined to "walk the path between worlds," and to "defend the balance against the encroaching shadows."

The words resonated with her, a chilling confirmation of her destiny. But they offered no concrete answers, no practical guidance. She felt a surge of frustration, a desperate need for clarity.

"Show me," she whispered, her voice echoing in the silent alcove. "Show me what I need to know."

As if in response, a faint light emanated from one of the books on the shelf. It was a small, unassuming volume, bound in plain leather, its title obscured by age and dust. Intrigued, Yuna reached for it, her fingers trembling slightly.

As she touched the book, a jolt of energy surged through her, a familiar sensation that resonated with the power within her. She pulled the book from the shelf and carefully opened it.

The pages were filled with handwritten notes, sketches, and diagrams, written in a script that seemed both familiar and alien. It was the handwriting of her ancestor, the Arithmancer of Numbers.

Yuna felt a surge of connection, a sudden understanding that transcended time and space. She could almost hear her ancestor's voice, whispering in her ear, guiding her through the intricate workings of Arithmancy, revealing the secrets of the guardians.

The book contained a detailed explanation of the guardian's powers, their ability to manipulate the very fabric of reality, to bend the laws of physics to their will. It described the techniques for harnessing this power, the rituals for invoking it, the dangers of misusing it.

It also spoke of the encroaching shadows, the forces of chaos that constantly threatened to unravel the delicate balance of the world. It warned of a coming darkness, a time of trial and tribulation, when the guardians would be needed more than ever.

Yuna devoured the text, her mind racing, her heart pounding. She felt a sense of awe, of trepidation, of determination. She was no longer just a student preparing for an exam. She was a guardian being awakened, a warrior being armed.

As she read, she noticed a small, folded piece of parchment tucked between the pages. She carefully unfolded it, revealing a map. It was a map of the academy, but with several locations marked with cryptic symbols.

Yuna recognized some of the locations: the library, the practice chambers, the gardens. But others were unfamiliar, hidden places she had never seen before.

Beneath the map was a single line of text: "The keys lie hidden where the numbers sing."

Yuna stared at the map, her mind buzzing with possibilities. What were these keys? What secrets did they unlock? And what did it mean for the numbers to sing?

She knew that she had to find those keys, to unlock those secrets. She had to prepare for the coming darkness, to protect the academy, to fulfill her destiny as a guardian.

But she also knew that she had to be careful. She couldn't trust anyone. She had to keep her true identity hidden, to maintain the facade of the ordinary student.

The path ahead was fraught with danger, but Yuna was no longer afraid. She had a purpose, a mission, a destiny to fulfill. And she would not rest until she had accomplished it.

With newfound resolve, she carefully closed the book, returned it to its place on the shelf, and slipped the map into her pocket. She left the library, her mind filled with the secrets she had uncovered, her heart burning with the fire of a guardian.

The next morning, the academy buzzed with nervous anticipation. The day of the Arithmetic Exam had finally arrived. Students milled about, their faces pale, their hands trembling. Some were frantically reviewing their notes, while others were simply staring blankly ahead, lost in their own anxious thoughts.

Yuna watched them, a sense of detachment washing over her. She was no longer just one of them, a student struggling to pass an exam. She was something more, something different. She carried a secret, a burden, a destiny that set her apart from the rest.

She tried to blend in, to maintain the illusion of normalcy. She wore her usual uniform, a simple grey robe. She carried her textbooks and notes, just like everyone else. She even forced a nervous smile for Callum , who greeted her with concerned looks.

"You okay, Yuna?" Callum asked, his brow furrowed with worry. "You look a little pale."

"I'm fine," Yuna replied, her voice a little strained. "Just a little nervous about the exam."

"Don't worry," Kael said,(poping out of nowhere) "You'll do great. You always do."

Yuna managed a weak smile. "Thanks, Kai."(Kael's nickname)

She knew that they were just trying to be supportive, but their words felt hollow, almost meaningless. They couldn't possibly understand what she was going through, the turmoil that was raging inside her.

As they walked towards the examination hall, Yuna couldn't help but feel a sense of isolation. She was surrounded by people, but she was completely alone. She was carrying a secret that she couldn't share, a burden that she had to bear on her own.

The examination hall was a vast, imposing room, filled with rows upon rows of desks. The air was thick with tension, the silence broken only by the nervous shuffling of feet and the occasional cough.

The students took their seats, their eyes fixed on the front of the hall. Master Elara stood at the podium, her face stern, her presence commanding.

"Welcome," she said, her voice echoing through the hall. "Today, you will be tested on your knowledge of Arithmancy, your ability to apply its principles, and your understanding of its underlying theories."

She paused, her gaze sweeping across the room. "This exam is not just a measure of your academic abilities. It is also a test of your character, your integrity, and your dedication to the pursuit of knowledge."

She held up a stack of scrolls. "These scrolls contain the questions that you will be answering. You will have three hours to complete the exam. You may use any materials that you have brought with you, but you may not communicate with each other in any way."

She distributed the scrolls, her movements precise, her expression unwavering. Yuna took her scroll, her fingers trembling slightly. She unrolled it and began to read.

The questions were challenging, but not impossible. They covered a wide range of topics, from basic arithmetic to advanced calculus, from simple equations to complex theorems.

Yuna approached the exam with a calm, focused mind. She reviewed the questions carefully, identified the key concepts, and formulated her answers with precision and clarity.

She worked steadily, methodically, ignoring the nervous fidgeting of the other students. She felt a sense of detachment, as if she were observing herself from a distance.

She solved the problems accurately, but not spectacularly. She demonstrated her understanding, but not her full potential. She walked the tightrope between competence and discretion, careful not to reveal too much.

As she worked, she couldn't help but think about the map she had found in the library. The keys, the secrets, the coming darkness. She knew that she couldn't ignore her destiny, that she had to prepare for the challenges that lay ahead.

But she also knew that she had to be patient, that she had to bide her time. She couldn't afford to rush into things, to draw attention to herself. She had to wait for the right moment, the right opportunity.

She finished the exam with time to spare. She reviewed her answers one last time, making sure that she hadn't made any careless mistakes. Then, she carefully rolled up her scroll and handed it to Master Mayfinder.

He took the scroll, her gaze lingering on Yuna for a moment. Yuna met his gaze, trying to convey a message of trust, of understanding, of shared responsibility.

Mayfinder nodded imperceptibly, his expression unreadable. Yuna turned and left the examination hall, her heart pounding, her mind racing.

The exam was over, but her journey had just begun.

The hours that followed the exam were a blur of uncertainty and anticipation. The students, freed from the immediate pressure of the test, buzzed with speculation and anxiety. They dissected the questions, compared answers, and agonized over their performance.

Yuna tried to avoid the frenzy, seeking refuge in the academy gardens. She wandered through the tranquil paths, trying to clear her mind, to focus on the tasks that lay ahead.

She knew that she couldn't wait for the results of the exam. She had to start preparing for the coming darkness, to find the keys, to unlock the secrets.

She pulled the map from her pocket and studied it carefully. The cryptic symbols seemed to shimmer in the sunlight, their meaning tantalizingly out of reach.

"The keys lie hidden where the numbers sing," she murmured, repeating the cryptic line from the library.

What did it mean for the numbers to sing? Was it a literal reference to music? Or was it a metaphor for something else?

She thought about the Arithmancy of music, the mathematical relationships between musical notes, the harmonies and dissonances that created melodies and rhythms.

Was she supposed to find a place where music was played? Or was she supposed to find a place where the principles of Arithmancy were expressed in a musical way?

She considered the academy's music hall, a grand auditorium where students practiced their instruments and performed for audiences. It was a long shot, but it was worth investigating.

She made her way to the music hall, her heart pounding with anticipation. The hall was empty, the silence broken only by the faint echo of her footsteps.

She walked through the rows of seats, her eyes scanning the stage, the walls, the ceiling. She saw nothing out of the ordinary, nothing that suggested a hidden key or a secret passage.

She climbed onto the stage, her gaze sweeping over the instruments that were arranged there: a harp, a lute, a flute, a violin.

She touched the strings of the harp, plucking them gently. The notes resonated through the hall, creating a haunting melody.

She listened carefully, trying to discern any hidden message, any subtle clue. But she heard nothing, only the pure, unadulterated sound of the music.

She sighed, her shoulders slumping with disappointment. She had hoped that the music hall would be the answer, but it seemed that she was mistaken.

She was about to leave when she noticed something out of the corner of her eye. It was a small, unassuming plaque on the wall behind the stage.

She approached the plaque and read the inscription: "In harmony with the universe, we find the key to understanding."

Yuna stared at the plaque, her mind racing. "In harmony with the universe..." Could it be?

She thought about the celestial spheres, the planets and stars that moved in perfect harmony, governed by the laws of physics. She thought about the Arithmancy of celestial bodies, the mathematical relationships between their movements, the cycles and patterns that shaped the cosmos.

Was she supposed to find a place where the celestial spheres were represented? A place where the Arithmancy of the cosmos was expressed?

She knew of only one place in the academy that fit that description: the observatory.

The observatory was a towering structure located on the highest point of the academy. It housed a powerful telescope and a collection of celestial charts and models.

Yuna had visited the observatory many times, fascinated by the beauty and complexity of the cosmos. She had spent hours gazing through the telescope, marveling at the distant stars and planets.

She made her way to the observatory, her heart pounding with renewed hope. The climb was arduous, the stairs winding and steep. But she didn't give up, fueled by the possibility that she was finally on the right track.

She reached the top of the observatory, her breath coming in ragged gasps. She pushed open the heavy door and stepped inside.

The observatory was bathed in soft, ethereal light, filtered through the massive dome that covered the building. The telescope loomed in the center of the room, its lens pointed towards the heavens.

Yuna walked towards the telescope, her eyes scanning the surroundings. She saw charts of constellations, models of planets, and diagrams of the solar system.

She studied the charts carefully, trying to decipher any hidden message, any subtle clue. But she saw nothing out of the ordinary, nothing that suggested a hidden key or a secret passage.

She approached the telescope and peered through the lens. She saw the moon, its surface scarred with craters and mountains. She saw the planets, their colors vibrant and distinct. She saw the stars, their light twinkling across vast distances.

She felt a sense of awe, of wonder, of connection to the universe. She was a tiny speck in the vastness of space, but she was also an integral part of it.

She lowered her eye from the lens and sighed, her shoulders slumping with disappointment. She had hoped that the observatory would be the answer, but it seemed that she was mistaken.

She was about to leave when she noticed something out of the corner of her eye. It was a small, unassuming model of the solar system, sitting on a table in the corner of the room.

She approached the model and examined it closely. It was a beautifully crafted replica of the sun, the planets, and their moons, all arranged in their proper positions.

She noticed that each planet was inscribed with a number, representing its distance from the sun.

She looked at the numbers more closely, her mind racing. She recognized them as the planetary constants, the mathematical values that defined the orbits of the planets.

She realized that the numbers were singing, not with sound, but with mathematics. They were expressing the underlying harmony of the solar system, the Arithmancy of the cosmos.

Yuna felt a surge of excitement, a sudden understanding that she was finally on the right track. She knew that the key was hidden somewhere within the model.

She examined the model more carefully, her fingers tracing the orbits of the planets. She noticed that one of the planets, Jupiter, was slightly out of alignment.

She gently pushed Jupiter back into its proper position, and as she did so, she heard a faint click.

She looked at the base of the model and saw that a small compartment had opened, revealing a key.

Yuna reached for the key, her fingers trembling with anticipation. It was a small, silver key, engraved with a cryptic symbol.

She held the key in her hand, her heart pounding with excitement. She had found the first key, the first piece of the puzzle.

But what did it unlock? And what secrets did it reveal? She will have to find out!

The silver key felt cool against her skin, a tangible link to her hidden legacy. As she held it, Yuna scanned the observatory once more, her mind racing. Where could this key possibly lead? The map mentioned hidden places, locations she had never seen before. Could one of them be behind a locked door somewhere in the academy?

A sudden thought struck her. The library. It was the heart of the academy, a repository of ancient knowledge and forgotten secrets. And she knew there were sections of the library that were off-limits to ordinary students, restricted archives accessible only to the highest-ranking faculty. Could one of those archives be the key's destination?

It was worth a shot. Slipping back into the shadows, Yuna made her way back to the library, her silver key safely tucked away. The library, bathed in the soft glow of enchanted lamps, seemed even more mysterious and imposing than usual. The towering shelves stretched into the darkness, filled with countless volumes, each holding untold stories and secrets. She continued her search for what felt like hours and just 30 minutes passed on the library's clock to midnight (that time she stopped searching for anymore secrets about the key even if she was a micrometre close, she thought of not doing it anymore cause she had really odd thoughts like what if the keys will bring Aakari here soo poor Yuna stopped the adventure she really wanted to find the mystery of).

Besides she just met callum who she trusted her whole life with but she herself didn't know why she was restraing herself from saying.She sat beside him half serious and half ummm........ with her thought of her liking Callum. After a while callum got bored of yuna simply Staring at two pages the arithmatic text book for like an hour after the last exam while he had been reading a normal novel. so he asked ' Are you okay ? ' and then finally Yuna decided to tell her whole story till now (Exept the Adventure).

After he listned to the unexplainable theory Yuna was going through very patiently. his tounge slipped and he said " So, you're my princess" instead of " So, you're a princess" (And that made an awkwardly silent moment between the two and both were flushing red). Yuna broke the silence and corrected that by saying " A guardion of Eldoria with royal blood, and making sure not to tell anyone exept Kael cause i can't he is in the boys dormiratory, Byee" and turned around and started running towards the end leaving Callum stuck thinking about her for the whole night forgetting that he was in the library.

Yuna was no less as soon as she the common room in the girls dormitory she was squeling (not that loud but IDK why but she was acting like a ghost was possesing her) the noise woke up Elara who was snoring her head on a scroll and her hand holding a pen and there was a heavy arithmatic book wide open on the floor. Yuna who had not noticed her fell off of her stool due to shoak almost landing at the fire place.

Elara then went and helped her in picking the books Yuna dropped along with herself and said her to stop squeling and both joined in reviewing their answers.

CHAPTER XV

The Revelations

The ancient room was dimly lit, with only a few flickering torches to illuminate the space. Yuna, Callum, and Kael stood in a circle, their eyes fixed on the intricate spellbook that lay open on a pedestal before them. They were about to attempt a powerful spell, one that would either seal Aakari away for good or unleash him if they failed. The weight of their task hung in the air, and the three friends could feel the tension building within them.

they (reffering to the trio practising after Callum and Yuna got over the awkward moment that happend the previous night) began to chant the words of the spell, their voices rose and fell in unison. The air around them began to vibrate with magical energy, and the torches on the walls flickered in response. Suddenly, a voice echoed through the room, making the three friends jump in surprise.

"Puny little kids practising to blow me away," Aakari's voice cackled, his tone dripping with malice. "You think you can defeat me? I am a being of great power, and you are nothing but mere children playing at magic."

Yuna's eyes flashed with determination as she raised her staff to protect her friends. The wood glowed with a soft, white light, and a barrier of energy erupted from the staff, surrounding the three friends. Callum, meanwhile, raised his hands, and a defensive wind began to blow around them, whipping their hair back and forth. Kael, not to be outdone, summoned a powerful water current, which swirled around the trio, protecting them from any potential attacks.

The three friends stood firm, their magic intertwining as they prepared to face whatever dangers lay ahead. But despite their bravery, Aakari's voice seemed to be coming from all around them, echoing off the walls and ceiling. It was as if he was everywhere and nowhere at the same time, making it impossible for them to pinpoint his location.

"You may have power," Aakari's voice sneered, "but you lack experience. You are no match for me, and soon you will be nothing but pawns in my game of power."

As the voice continued to taunt them, the three friends began to feel a creeping sense of doubt. What if they weren't strong enough? What if they failed to seal Aakari away? The fear of failure threatened to overwhelm them, but they knew they couldn't give in. They had to keep pushing forward, no matter what.

With renewed determination, Yuna, Callum, and Kael focused their energy and launched a combined attack. The air was filled with the sound of rushing water, howling wind, and crackling lightning as the three friends unleashed their magic. The room shook and trembled, and the torches on the walls flickered wildly as the energy built to a crescendo.

But just as it seemed like their combined attack was about to hit its mark, Aakari slipped from their grasp. The voice stopped laughing, and the room fell silent. The three friends stood panting, their chests heaving with exertion, as they realized that their enemy had vanished.

The silence was oppressive, and the three friends exchanged worried glances. They had been so sure that they had him cornered, but Aakari had managed to slip away once again. The weight of their failure hung in the air, and for a moment, they just stood there, unsure of what to do next.

Finally, Yuna spoke up, her voice barely above a whisper. "We need to sit down and regroup. We can't keep going on like this."

Callum and Kael nodded in agreement, and the three friends sank to the ground, exhausted. They sat in silence for a moment, trying to catch their breath and process what had just happened.

As they sat there, Yuna began to speak, her voice filled with a newfound determination. "We can't give up. We have to keep pushing forward, no matter what. We owe it to ourselves, to each other, and to the world to stop Aakari."

Callum and Kael nodded in agreement, and the three friends began to discuss their next move. They knew that they had to come up with a new plan, one that would take into account Aakari's cunning and power. They couldn't just keep reacting to his attacks; they needed to take the initiative and come up with a strategy that would allow them to defeat him once and for all.

As they talked, the three friends began to feel a sense of hope that they hadn't felt in a long time. They knew that the road ahead would be difficult, but they were ready to face whatever challenges lay in store. They were ready to face Aakari, and they were determined to emerge victorious.

The darkness outside seemed to press in around them, but the three friends didn't let it intimidate them. They knew that they had each other, and that together, they could overcome anything. They were a team, a trio of young wizards who were determined to save the world from the forces of darkness.

As they sat there, planning and scheming, the three friends began to feel a sense of excitement building within them. They knew that the final faceoff with Aakari was approaching, and they were ready. They were ready to put everything on the line, to risk it all, and to emerge victorious.

The ancient room seemed to grow quieter, as if it too was waiting with bated breath for the outcome of the impending battle. The torches on the walls flickered softly, casting eerie shadows on the walls as the three friends continued to plan and prepare.

And then, just as they were about to come up with a final plan, a faint whispering began to echo through the room. It was a soft, raspy voice, one that seemed to be coming from all around them.

"The time of reckoning is near," the voice whispered. "The final battle approaches. Are you prepared to face what lies ahead?"

The three friends exchanged nervous glances, their hearts pounding in their chests. They knew that the voice was right; the time of reckoning was indeed near. They were about to face their greatest challenge yet, and they weren't sure if they were ready.

But they knew they had to try. They had to face whatever lay ahead, no matter how daunting it seemed. They had to be brave, to be strong, and to trust in each other.

With a deep breath, Yuna stood up, her eyes flashing with determination. "We're ready," she said, her voice firm and resolute. "We're ready to face whatever lies ahead."

Callum and Kael nodded in agreement, and the three friends stood up, their faces set with determination. They knew that the road ahead would be difficult, but they were ready to face it head-on. They were ready to face Aakari, and they were determined to emerge victorious.

The whispering voice seemed to fade away, leaving the three friends standing in silence. But they knew that they weren't alone. They knew that the ancient room was watching them, waiting to see what they would do next.

And with that knowledge, the three friends set their faces towards the future, ready to face whatever lay ahead. They were ready to face the darkness, to face Aakari, and to emerge victorious. They were ready to save the world, and they were determined to do it together.

As they stood there, the torches on the walls seemed to flicker in approval, casting a warm glow over the three friends. The ancient room seemed to nod in agreement, its secrets and mysteries waiting to be unlocked by the brave and determined trio.

And with that, the three friends took their first step towards the final faceoff with Aakari. They took their first step towards destiny, towards a future that was uncertain but full of promise. They took their first step towards saving the world, and they were ready to face whatever lay ahead.

The journey ahead would be long and difficult, but the three friends were ready. They were ready to face the challenges that lay ahead, to overcome the obstacles that stood in their way, and to emerge victorious. They were ready to save the world, and they were determined to do it together.

As they stood there, the darkness outside seemed to press in around them, but the three friends didn't let it intimidate them. They knew that they had each other, and that together, they could overcome anything. They were a team, a trio of young wizards who were determined to save the world from the forces of darkness.

And with that knowledge, they set off towards the final faceoff with Aakari, ready to face whatever lay ahead. They were ready to save the world, and they were determined to do it together.

The ancient room seemed to whisper its approval, its secrets and mysteries waiting to be unlocked by the brave and determined trio. The torches on the walls flickered softly, casting a warm glow over the three friends as they set off towards their destiny.

And as they walked, the darkness outside seemed to recede, pushed back by the light of their determination and bravery. The three friends walked tall, their hearts full of hope and their spirits unbroken. They walked towards the future, towards a world that was full of promise and possibility.

And as they walked, the ancient room seemed to fade away, its secrets and mysteries waiting to be unlocked by the brave and determined trio. The torches on the walls flickered one last time, and then went out, plunging the room into darkness.

But the three friends didn't need the light of the torches to guide them. They had each other, and they had their determination and bravery. They had their magic, and they had their hearts.

And with that, they set off towards the final faceoff with Aakari, ready to face whatever lay ahead. They were ready to save the world, and they were determined to do it together.

The journey ahead would be long and difficult, but the three friends were ready. They were ready to face the challenges that lay ahead, to overcome the obstacles that stood in their way, and to emerge victorious. They were ready to save the world, and they were determined to do it together.

And as they walked, the darkness outside seemed to recede, pushed back by the light of their determination and bravery. The three friends walked tall, their hearts full of hope and their spirits unbroken. They walked towards the future, towards a world that was full of promise and possibility.

The final faceoff with Aakari was approaching, and the three friends were ready. They were ready to face whatever lay ahead, to overcome the challenges that stood in their way, and to emerge victorious. They were ready to save the world, and they were determined to do it together.

And with that knowledge, they set off towards their destiny, ready to face whatever lay ahead. They were ready to save the world, and they were determined to do it together.

The ancient room was gone, but its secrets and mysteries would stay with the three friends forever. The torches on the walls were extinguished, but the light of their determination and bravery would guide them through the darkness.

And as they walked, the three friends knew that they would always stand together, no matter what lay ahead. They would always have each other's backs, and they would always be ready to face whatever challenges came their way.

The final faceoff with Aakari was approaching, and the three friends were ready. They were ready to face whatever lay ahead, to overcome the challenges that stood in their way, and to emerge victorious. They were ready to save the world, and they were determined to do it together.

And with that knowledge, they set off towards their destiny, ready to face whatever lay ahead. They were ready to save the world, and they were determined to do it together.

The journey ahead would be long and difficult, but the three friends were ready. They were ready to face the challenges that lay ahead, to overcome the obstacles that stood in their way, and to emerge victorious. They were ready to save the world, and they were determined to do it together.

And as they walked, the darkness outside seemed to recede, pushed back by the light of their determination and bravery. The three friends walked tall, their hearts full of hope and their spirits unbroken. They walked towards the future, towards a world that was full of promise and possibility.

The final faceoff with Aakari was approaching, and the three friends were ready. They were ready to face whatever lay ahead, to overcome the challenges that stood in their way, and to emerge victorious. They were ready to save the world, and they were determined to do it together.

And with that knowledge, they set off towards their destiny, ready to face whatever lay ahead. They were ready to save the world, and they were determined to do it together.

The ancient room was gone, but its secrets and mysteries would stay with the three friends forever. The torches on the walls were extinguished, but the light of their determination and bravery would guide them through the darkness.

And as they walked, the three friends knew that they would always stand together, no matter what lay ahead. They would always have each other's backs, and they would always be ready to face whatever challenges came their way.

The final faceoff with Aakari was approaching, and the three friends were ready. They were ready to face whatever lay ahead, to overcome the challenges that stood in their way, and to emerge victorious. They were ready to save the world, and they were determined to do it together.

And with that knowledge, they set off towards their destiny, ready to face whatever lay ahead. They were ready to save the world, and they were determined to do it together.

The journey ahead would be long and difficult, but the three friends were ready. They were ready to face the challenges that lay ahead, to overcome the obstacles that stood in their way, and to emerge victorious. They were ready to save the world, and they were determined to do it together.

And as they walked, the darkness outside seemed to recede, pushed back by the light of their determination and bravery. The three friends walked tall, their hearts full of hope and their spirits unbroken. They walked towards the future, towards a world that was full of promise and possibility.

The final faceoff with Aakari was approaching, and the three friends were ready. They were ready to face whatever lay ahead, to overcome the challenges that stood in their way, and to emerge victorious. They were ready to save the world, and they were determined to do it together.

And with that knowledge, they set off towards their destiny, ready to face whatever lay ahead. They were ready to save the world, and they were determined to do it together.

The ancient room was gone, but its secrets and mysteries would stay with the three friends forever. The torches on the walls were extinguished, but the light of their determination and bravery would guide them through the darkness.

And as they walked, the three friends knew that they would always stand together, no matter what lay ahead. They would always have each other's backs, and they would always be ready to face whatever challenges came their way.

The final faceoff with Aakari was approaching, and the three friends were ready. They were ready to face whatever lay ahead, to overcome the challenges that stood in their way, and to emerge victorious. They were ready to save the world, and they were determined to do it together.

And with that knowledge, they set off towards their destiny, ready to face whatever lay ahead. They were ready to save the world, and they were determined to do it together.

The journey ahead would be long and difficult, but the three friends were ready. They were ready to face the challenges that lay ahead, to overcome the obstacles that stood in their way, and to emerge victorious. They were ready to save the world, and they were determined to do it together.

And as they walked, the darkness outside seemed to recede, pushed back by the light of their determination and bravery. The three friends walked tall, their hearts full of hope and their spirits unbroken. They walked towards the future, towards a world that was full of promise and possibility.

The final faceoff with Aakari was approaching, and the three friends were ready. They were ready to face whatever lay ahead, to overcome the challenges that stood in their way, and to emerge victorious. They were ready to save the world, and they were determined to do it together.

And with that knowledge, they set off towards their destiny, ready to face whatever lay ahead. They were ready to save the world, and they were determined to do it together.

The ancient room was gone, but its secrets and mysteries would stay with the three friends forever. The torches on the walls were extinguished, but the light of their determination and bravery would guide them through the darkness.

And as they walked, the three friends knew that they would always stand together, no matter what lay ahead. They would always have each other's backs, and they would always be ready to face whatever challenges came their way.

The final faceoff with Aakari was approaching, and the three friends were ready. They were ready to face whatever lay ahead, to overcome the challenges that stood in their way, and to emerge victorious. They were ready to save the world, and they were determined to do it together.

And with that knowledge, they set off towards their destiny, ready to face whatever lay ahead. They were ready to save the world, and they were determined to do it together.

The journey ahead would be long and difficult, but the three friends were ready. They were ready to face the challenges that lay ahead, to overcome the obstacles that stood in their way, and to emerge victorious. They were ready to save the world, and they were determined to do it together.

And as they walked, the darkness outside seemed to recede, pushed back by the light of their determination and bravery. The three friends walked tall, their hearts full of hope and their spirits unbroken. They walked towards the future, towards a world that was full of promise and possibility.

The final faceoff with Aakari was approaching, and the three friends were ready. They were ready to face whatever lay ahead, to overcome the challenges that stood in their way, and to emerge victorious. They were ready to save the world, and they were determined to do it together.

And with that knowledge, they set off towards their destiny, ready to face whatever lay ahead. They were ready to save the world, and they were determined to do it together.

The ancient room was gone, but its secrets and mysteries would stay with the three friends forever. The torches on the walls were extinguished, but the light of their determination and bravery would guide them through the darkness.

And as they walked, the three friends knew that they would always stand together, no matter what lay ahead. They would always have each other's backs, and they would always be ready to face whatever challenges came their way.

The final faceoff with Aakari was approaching, and the three friends were ready. They were ready to face whatever lay ahead, to overcome the challenges that stood in their way, and to emerge victorious. They were ready to save

CHAPTER XVI

Choices and Consequences

The air was thick with tension as Yuna stood at the edge of the grand hall, her eyes fixed on the figure of Aakari, who loomed before her. The dark sorcerer's presence seemed to fill the entire space, his malevolent energy pulsing like a living thing. Yuna's heart pounded in her chest, her mind racing with the weight of the choices that lay before her.

To her left stood Kael, his eyes burning with a fierce determination, his hand on the hilt of his sword. Beside him, the wizard, Zephyr, watched Aakari with a calculating gaze, his fingers steepled together in a gesture of quiet contemplation. On her right, the young prince, Arin, stood tall, his jaw set in a firm line, his eyes flashing with a mix of fear and resolve.

Yuna's thoughts turned to the journey that had brought her to this moment. She had begun as a simple, orphaned girl, living on the streets of the kingdom. But the discovery of her royal bloodline had changed everything. She had been thrust into a world of magic and politics, forced to navigate the treacherous landscape of Eldoria's nobility.

As she looked out at the faces of her friends, Yuna felt a surge of gratitude and love. They had stood by her, supported her, and helped her to grow into the strong, capable woman she was today. But with Aakari's return, Yuna was faced with a daunting reality: the fate of Eldoria hung in the balance, and the choices she made would have far-reaching consequences.

Aakari, sensing her gaze, turned to face her. His eyes, like two black holes, seemed to bore into her very soul, searching for any weakness or fear. Yuna stood tall, refusing to back down, even as her heart trembled with anticipation.

"So, Yuna," Aakari said, his voice low and menacing. "I see you have gathered your little friends around you. How quaint. How...

amusing."

Yuna's anger flared at the sorcerer's mocking tone, but she bit back her retort, knowing that she had to keep her wits about her. Aakari was a master manipulator, and she couldn't afford to let him get under her skin.

"We are not afraid of you, Aakari," Yuna said, her voice steady and firm. "We will not back down. You have brought darkness and destruction to our land, and it is time for you to pay the price."

Aakari chuckled, the sound sending a shiver down Yuna's spine. "Oh, Yuna. You are so predictable. You think you can defeat me? I have the power of the ancient magic at my command. I have the support of the shadow creatures, and the loyalty of the dark elves. You, on the other hand, have... what? A handful of misfits and a few rusty swords?"

Yuna felt a sting from Aakari's words, but she refused to let him get to her. She knew that she had something that Aakari did not: the love and support of her friends, and the power of her own inner strength.

"We may not have your power, Aakari," Yuna said, "but we have something that you will never have: our hearts, our souls, and our determination to protect our land and our people. You may have the magic, but we have the courage, and that is what will ultimately decide the fate of Eldoria."

Aakari sneered, his face twisting in contempt. "Courage? Ha! Courage is just a word, a fleeting emotion. It is nothing compared to the power of the ancient magic. And as for your little friends... they are nothing but pawns, waiting to be sacrificed on the altar of my ambition."

Yuna felt a surge of anger at Aakari's words, but she knew that she had to keep her cool. She glanced at her friends, seeing the determination in their eyes, and knew that she was not alone.

"We will not back down, Aakari," Yuna said, her voice firm. "We will fight you, with every ounce of strength we have. And we will win, because we have something that you do not: the power of our friendship, and the love that we share."

Aakari laughed, the sound echoing through the hall. "We shall see about that, Yuna. We shall see about that. But for now... let us end this farce. Let us see who is the stronger, you or I."

With a wave of his hand, Aakari summoned a dark and swirling vortex, a portal to a realm of shadow and darkness. Yuna felt a shiver run down her spine as she realized that Aakari was challenging her to a duel, a battle of magic and wits that would decide the fate of Eldoria.

Yuna hesitated, unsure of what to do. She knew that she was no match for Aakari's power, not in a straight-up fight. But she also knew that she couldn't back down, not now, not when the fate of her land and her people hung in the balance.

As she looked at her friends, Yuna saw the fear and uncertainty in their eyes. They were waiting for her to make a decision, to lead them into battle. And in that moment, Yuna knew what she had to do.

"I accept your challenge, Aakari," Yuna said, her voice firm and resolute. "I will face you, alone and unafraid. And I will emerge victorious, because I have the power of my friends, and the love of my land, to guide me."

Aakari smiled, his eyes glinting with amusement. "We shall see about that, Yuna. We shall see about that. But for now... let us begin our little game. Let us see who will emerge victorious, and who will fall to the darkness."

With a wave of his hand, Aakari stepped through the portal, disappearing into the shadows. Yuna felt a surge of fear, but she steeled herself, knowing that she had to follow him, no matter the cost.

"I'll go with you," Kael said, stepping forward, his sword at the ready.

"No, Kael," Yuna said, shaking her head. "This is my fight, my destiny. I must face Aakari alone."

Kael's face fell, but he nodded, understanding in his eyes. "I'll be here, waiting for you. We all will."

Yuna smiled, feeling a sense of gratitude and love for her friends. She knew that she could count on them, no matter what.

With a deep breath, Yuna stepped through the portal, following Aakari into the unknown. The darkness swallowed her whole, and she felt herself being pulled into a realm of shadow and magic, where the very fabric of reality seemed to bend and twist.

As she walked, Yuna felt a sense of trepidation growing inside her. She knew that she was walking into a trap, that Aakari had planned this duel to his advantage. But she also knew that she had to see it through, no matter the cost.

The path twisted and turned, leading Yuna deeper into the heart of the shadow realm. She could feel the weight of Aakari's magic bearing down on her, trying to crush her spirit and break her will. But Yuna refused to give in, drawing on the power of her friends, and the love of her land, to guide her forward.

Finally, after what seemed like an eternity, Yuna saw a glimmer of light in the distance. She quickened her pace, her heart pounding with anticipation, and emerged into a vast, cavernous space, lit by a thousand flickering torches.

Aakari stood at the far end of the cavern, his eyes blazing with malevolent energy. Yuna felt a shiver run down her spine as she realized that she was face to face with her greatest enemy, the one who had brought darkness and destruction to her land.

"So, Yuna," Aakari said, his voice echoing off the walls of the cavern. "We meet again. And this time, only one of us will emerge victorious."

Yuna stood tall, her heart pounding with fear and anticipation. She knew that she was in for the fight of her life, but she was ready. She was ready to face Aakari, to defeat him, and to save her land from the brink of destruction.

The battle began, with Aakari summoning a wave of dark magic that threatened to consume Yuna whole. But Yuna was not alone, and she drew on the power of her friends, and the love of her land, to guide her forward.

The fight was fierce and intense, with both Yuna and Aakari exchanging blows and counterattacks. Yuna felt herself being pushed to the limit, her magic and her strength being tested to the breaking point. But she refused to give in, drawing on every ounce of courage and determination she possessed.

As the battle raged on, Yuna began to feel a sense of hope growing inside her. She was holding her own against Aakari, and she knew that she had the power to defeat him. But just as she thought she was gaining the upper hand, Aakari unleashed a devastating blast of magic that sent Yuna flying across the cavern.

Yuna struggled to get back to her feet, her body aching and her magic depleted. She knew that she was running out of time, and that she had to end the battle quickly, before Aakari could deliver the final blow.

With a surge of adrenaline, Yuna launched herself at Aakari, determined to defeat him once and for all. The two enemies clashed, their magic and their strength locked in a fierce and deadly struggle.

In the end, it was Yuna who emerged victorious, her magic and her courage proving to be too much for Aakari to handle. The dark sorcerer let out a defeated cry, and fell to the ground, his body broken and his magic spent.

Yuna stood over him, her chest heaving with exhaustion, her magic depleted. She knew that she had saved her land, and that she had fulfilled her destiny. But as she looked down at Aakari, she felt a sense of sadness and regret. She had hoped that he would see the error of his ways, and that he would turn away from the darkness. But it was too late for that now.

With a heavy heart, Yuna turned and walked away, leaving Aakari to his fate. She knew that she would never forget the lessons she had learned, and that she would always carry the scars of the battle with her. But she also knew that she had emerged stronger, and that she was ready to face whatever challenges lay ahead.

As she stepped back through the portal, Yuna was greeted by the warm smiles of her friends, who had been waiting anxiously for her return. They cheered and congratulated her, hailing her as a hero, and Yuna felt a sense of pride and satisfaction. She had saved her land, and she had fulfilled her destiny.

But as she looked out at the faces of her friends, Yuna knew that she had also learned something important. She had learned that true strength came not from magic or power, but from the love and support of those around her. And she knew that she would always cherish the bonds of friendship that had carried her through the darkest of times.

The fate of Eldoria was secure, and Yuna had emerged victorious. But as she walked away from the portal, Yuna knew that she would never forget the choices she had made, and the consequences that had followed. She had chosen to stand up for what she believed in, and she had chosen to fight for her land and her people. And in the end, she had emerged victorious, her heart full of love and her spirit full of courage.

The journey had been long and difficult, but Yuna had made it through, and she had emerged stronger and wiser. She had learned the value of friendship and the power of love, and she had discovered the true meaning of courage and determination. And as she walked away from the portal, Yuna knew that she would always carry the lessons of her journey with her, and that she would always be ready to face whatever challenges lay ahead.

The story of Yuna and her friends would be told and retold for generations to come, a reminder of the power of courage and determination, and the importance of standing up for what is right. And as the years passed, Yuna's legend would grow, inspiring countless others to follow in her footsteps, and to fight for their own lands and their own people.

But for now, Yuna was content to bask in the glow of her victory, surrounded by the friends she loved, and the land she had sworn to protect. She knew that she had made a difference, and that she had changed the course of history. And as she looked out at the bright future that lay ahead, Yuna knew that she would always be ready to face whatever challenges came her way, armed with the power of her courage, and the love of her friends.

In the aftermath of the battle, Yuna and her friends worked tirelessly to rebuild and restore the land. They used their unique skills and abilities to help those in need, and to bring hope and light to a world that had been plagued by darkness.

As they worked, Yuna couldn't help but think about the journey that had brought her to this moment. She thought about the people she had met, the challenges she had faced, and the lessons she had learned. And she knew that she would always be grateful for the experience, and for the friends she had made along the way.

One day, as Yuna was walking through the city, she came across a group of children playing in the street. They were laughing and chasing each other, completely carefree. Yuna watched them for a moment, a smile on her face. She remembered when she was their age, and how she had felt so lost and alone. But now, she was a hero, a champion of the land and its people.

As she continued on her way, Yuna felt a sense of pride and purpose. She knew that she had made a difference, and that she would always be remembered as a brave and courageous warrior. And she knew that she would always be ready to defend her land and her people, no matter what challenges lay ahead.

The years passed, and Yuna's legend grew. She became known throughout the land as a hero and a champion, a symbol of hope and courage in a world that often seemed dark and frightening. And though she faced many challenges and dangers, Yuna never wavered, always standing strong and true to her values and her principles.

One day, as Yuna was sitting on a hill overlooking the city, she saw a figure approaching her. It was an old man, with a long white beard and a twinkle in his eye. He walked up to Yuna and sat down beside her, looking out at the city below.

"Yuna," he said, his voice low and gravelly. "I have been watching you for a long time. I have seen the way you have dedicated your life to helping others, and the way you have stood up for what is right. And I must say, I am impressed."

Yuna turned to the old man, curious. "Who are you?" she asked.

"My name is not important," the old man replied. "What is important is the message I have come to bring you. Yuna, you have been given a great gift, the gift of courage and determination. And you have used that gift to make a real difference in the world. But now, it is time for you to pass that gift on to others."

Yuna was taken aback. "What do you mean?" she asked.

"The world is always in need of heroes," the old man said. "And it is time for you to find and train a new generation of warriors, people who will carry on your legacy and continue to fight for what is right. Will you do this, Yuna?"

Yuna thought for a moment, considering the old man's words. And then, with a sense of purpose and determination, she nodded. "Yes," she said. "I will do it. I will find and train a new generation of heroes, and I will make sure that your message is heard throughout the land."

The old man smiled, his eyes twinkling with approval. "I knew I could count on you, Yuna," he said. "You have always been a true hero, and now you will be a hero to a new generation of warriors. Go out there and make a difference, Yuna. The world is waiting for you."

And with that, the old man stood up and walked away, leaving Yuna to ponder the weight of his words. She knew that she had a great responsibility ahead of her, but she was ready. She was ready to face whatever challenges came her way, and to make a real difference in the world.

A New Dawn

As the last remnants of sunlight faded beyond the horizon, Yuna stood at the edge of the enchanted forest, her hands intertwined with Callum's. The warmth of his touch and the gentle pressure of his fingers wrapped around hers brought a sense of comfort and peace. It was a feeling she had grown accustomed to in the days following the battle against Aaravos. The darkness that had once threatened to consume their world had been vanquished, and with it, a new beginning had emerged.

Kael, ever the jokester, stood beside them, his quick wit and clever quips weaving a spell of laughter and joy around the trio. Yuna's eyes sparkled as she giggled at one of Kael's particularly clever jokes, the sound of her own laughter a balm to her soul. It was moments like these that reminded her of the beauty and wonder that still existed in their world, even in the face of adversity.

As they stood there, the setting sun casting a warm orange glow over the forest, Yuna felt a sense of reflection wash over her. The battle against Aaravos had left its scars, both physical and emotional. The memories of the darkness and the fear that had gripped their world still lingered, a reminder of the dangers that lay in the shadows. But even as the shadows persisted, Yuna knew that she and her friends had emerged stronger, their bond forged in the fire of adversity.

The days that followed the battle had been a time of healing and growth, a chance for Yuna to come to terms with the trauma she had faced. She had been forced to confront the depths of her own strength and resilience, and in doing so, had discovered a newfound sense of purpose. The experience had changed her, had tempered her like steel in the fire, and she knew that she would never be the same again.

As the stars began to twinkle in the night sky, Yuna felt a whisper of adventure beckoning her forward. The world was still full of mysteries and wonders, and she knew that she and her friends were ready to face whatever lay ahead. The shadows that lingered would always be a reminder of the dangers that existed, but they would not hold her back. With Callum by her side and Kael's jokes to guide her, Yuna knew that she was ready to embark on a new chapter, one that would be filled with excitement, danger, and discovery.

The enchanted forest, once a place of darkness and fear, now seemed to stretch out before her like an open road, full of possibilities and promise. Yuna took a deep breath, feeling the cool night air fill her lungs, and smiled. She knew that the journey ahead would not be easy, but she was ready. With her friends by her side, she was ready to face whatever lay in store, to laugh in the face of danger, and to forge a new path, one that would be filled with wonder, magic, and adventure. The whispers of the unknown beckoned her forward, and Yuna, with a sense of excitement and trepidation, stepped into the unknown, ready to begin her new journey.

Yuna's quest unfolds in "Echoes of Destiny" as ancient foes rise, and new allies emerge, testing her resolve against darkness in the mystical world of Eldoria suddenly.

www.ingramcontent.com/pod-product-compliance
Lightning Source LLC
Chambersburg PA
CBHW021205130726
47988CB00002B/516